FROZEN DREAM

TED GALDI

AETHON THRILLS

aethonbooks.com

FROZEN DREAM
©2023 TED GALDI

This book is protected under the copyright laws of the United States of America. No part of this publication may be reproduced, stored in a retrieval system, or transmitted, in any form or by any means, without the prior permission in writing of the publisher, nor be otherwise circulated in any form of binding or cover other than that in which it is published and without a similar condition including this condition being imposed on the subsequent purchaser. Any reproduction or unauthorized use of the material or artwork contained herein is prohibited without the express written permission of the authors.

Aethon Books supports the right to free expression and the value of copyright. The purpose of copyright is to encourage writers and artists to produce the creative works that enrich our culture.

The scanning, uploading, and distribution of this book without permission is a theft of the author's intellectual property. If you would like to use material from the book (other than for review purposes), please contact editor@aethonbooks.com. Thank you for your support of the author's rights.

Aethon Books
www.aethonbooks.com

Print, and eBook formatting and cover art by Steve Beaulieu.

Published by Aethon Books LLC.

Aethon Books is not responsible for websites (or their content) that are not owned by the publisher.

This book is a work of fiction. Names, characters, places, and incidents are the product of the author's imagination or are used fictitiously. Any resemblance to actual events, locales, or persons, living or dead is coincidental.

All rights reserved.

ALSO BY TED GALDI

<u>COLE MADDOX</u>

BLACK QUIET
RAZOR MOON
FROZEN DREAM

1

The forest where Cole Maddox hiked as a teenager looks different. A 39-ton hydraulic machine has sliced it up. He gazes at massive pieces of black steel pipe in a trench cut through the mountain, the January snow dotting them. Each is imprinted *Property of Stallos Energy Corporation.*

"It's about that time," a young laborer says. He tosses the bag of his packed lunch into a garbage can on the construction site and claps a couple times. "What do you say, Jay?" A few other guys clap, too.

After Stallos Energy gained approval to build a natural gas pipeline across the southwestern portion of Montana, it outsourced much of the development to local firms, including small Maddox Construction, which Cole runs with his brother Jay.

Cole, thirty-six, and Jay, forty, are from a generation before most of the laborers. When the project started, Jay would often give the twentysomethings unsolicited life advice. They began posting videos of him on TikTok, with the hashtag #whatdoyousayjay. Pudgy Jay pops one last potato chip into his mouth and struts to the head of the group.

"Does your brother know they're making fun of him?" asks site boss Ollie, who's in his early fifties, but looks at least sixty. Unlike most of the others on the mountain, he is a full-time Stallos Energy employee, the executive project engineer. His jeans, a bit baggy, billow over his scrawny legs in the wind.

"He knows," Cole says. "But he likes the attention."

"Kids on the internet watch this nonsense?"

"Jay's thoughts on neck tattoos were seen by something like fifty thousand people. His opinion on women with fake butts, triple."

Ollie shakes his head. "Scary to think where this country will be in ten years." He checks his watch. "They've got just a few more minutes of lunch break to giggle over this silly shit, then it's back to work." He walks to his pickup. Since smoking isn't allowed on the site, he drives a few hundred feet down the mountain to puff a cigarette multiple times a day.

"Welcome to another installment," the laborer recording Jay says. "Today's topic...man buns."

Jay tilts his head and rubs his chin, like a professor in thought. "You all out there might think a rugged guy like me would be anti-man-bun. Say they're for pansies. But, as you all know, I'm honest. Sometimes brutally so. Can I pull off a man bun? No. I don't have the hair texture. Or the bone structure. But on certain individuals, they can work." He points at Cole. "My baby brother over there, perfect example."

The guy videoing turns the camera to Cole.

"Look at my lil bro," Jay says. "Silky, dirty-blond locks, six foot two, face out of a magazine. Genetically, I got the Danny DeVito end of the stick. But that's all right. I've grown to accept it. Cole, how 'bout you pop the hardhat off and style that mane into a man bun for us?"

Cole, smiling, waves off the camera.

"Though he may look like a movie star," Jay says, "my baby

bro clearly lacks showmanship. You're letting down the good people out there."

"Let me just tie my boot," Cole says, "and I'll come right over." Cole bends down, but packs a snowball. He wings it at Jay, nailing his hardhat, pushing it half off his head. The laborers burst into laughter.

Smirking, Jay hurls a snowball at his brother. Cole ducks, the ball exploding against a pipe-lifting track hoe. Cole chases him. Jay jogs down a hill, out of sight.

"Suck ice," Jay shouts, jumping out from behind a tree. He tosses another snowball, which Cole sidesteps.

Cole winds up to return fire, but pauses when something in the brush catches his attention.

"What the hell you looking at?" Jay asks.

Cole lets go of the snowball and walks into the uncleared portion of woods bordering the site. The strong wind chills the side of his face. He moves an evergreen branch out of the way for a closer look.

Jay's boots crunch in the snow as he paces over. When he notices what Cole is staring at, he says, "Oh my God."

2

Over thirty construction workers huddle around Cole, trying to get a glimpse. A patch of snowy ground is stained red. Blood leaks from the body of a dead rabbit, hanging by its neck from a rope around a tree. The feet and ears hacked off, the tiny white remains sway in the wind.

"Enough with this *America's Funniest Home Videos* bullcrap," boss Ollie says, from up on the hill. "We've got a lot more pipe to get into the ground."

A laborer points him toward the rabbit. Ollie shoulders his way through the workers, up to Cole. He smells like Marlboros. When he sees the maimed animal, his eyes widen.

"Whoever did this clearly didn't want to get too close to the site, maybe knew we had cameras," Cole says. "But they definitely wanted us to notice."

"Devil worshippers," a worker says.

"Nah, bro," another replies. "I know exactly what this is. I watched a documentary all about it. Aliens."

"Get the hell out of here, dumbass."

"Look it up. Been going on for years. Aliens come down in spaceships and do screwy things to animals. Some cows get—"

"Jesus Christ," Ollie says. "I've been in this business for years. Weird stuff like this is common on natural gas sites. It's just environmentalists trying to send some message to make us feel guilty about killing trees or whatever. But it ain't really about that at all. They're just bitter because their lives suck. A bunch of losers upset 'cause the world is competitive and they don't stack up. They don't like companies like Stallos because we do stack up. These people are insignificant. Pay them no attention. Get back to work. C'mon."

The men disperse from the dead rabbit. Many seem disturbed. Yes, environmentalists tend to have grudges against fossil-fuel companies, however, they also claim to care about nature. Animals are a part of nature. Cutting up a rabbit for a gruesome display doesn't seem like something an environmentalist would do.

On his phone, Cole Googles "Hanging rabbit no ears feet." He scrolls through the results. A certain one is interesting.

In various European villages, during the Middle Ages, rabbits chopped up while still alive were considered symbols of corruption. The bodies were often hung outside the doors of merchants and politicians the townspeople viewed as unscrupulous. The pain the innocent, powerless animal felt was supposed to represent the pain the innocent, powerless villagers felt. Cole's stomach knots when he considers this rabbit could've suffered six brutal injuries, two ears and four feet, while still conscious.

As far as Cole knows, Stallos Energy is a legitimate corporation. Trading on the public stock exchange, it's exposed to intense scrutiny from the media. If Stallos was involved in some corruption scandal, for whatever reason, it didn't reach the news.

The workers return to their posts. Power saws, used to shape steel support brackets, fire up, their roar echoing through the forest. Cole, trying to push the image of the small, bloody animal body out of his head, jumps into the trench with Jay. They stand near the end of a piece of heavy-gauge double containment steel pipe, four feet in diameter, ten times that in length. They prepare to connect it to another piece as soon as it's lowered into the ground.

A pair of men wraps the propped-up piece in a heavy-duty sling attached to the arm of a track hoe. "I've heard some stuff about these environmentalist nuts," one of the guys says, above the sound of the power saws. "Some of them blow shit up, facts."

"Like what?" the second man asks.

The first slaps the pipe. "Like this. Maybe the bunny was just supposed to freak us out. But they got something a lot worse up their sleeve. Like, they stuck TNT somewhere in the pipes and they're watching us from a distance, ready to hit the detonator button."

The second man's expression tenses as he finishes setting up the sling. He flashes a thumbs-up to the guy operating the track hoe.

The truck's mechanical arm lifts. The forty-foot piece of pipe rises off its wooden-beam supports. It rocks in the snowy sky. A bit of rocking is common, however, the movement is more chaotic than that.

The sling seems to be a few feet off from the center. Distracted by a potential TNT blast, the loaders must've attached it wrong.

"Clear out," someone shouts.

The pipe's wobbling intensifies. All the workers in the trench backpedal from it, except Cole.

The track-hoe driver, his face panicky, attempts to lower the big cylinder of steel back onto its supports. It slams down onto one, knocking it over, a piece of wood shooting into the air. Guys scream and curse. The pipe topples out of the sling onto the sloped ground and begins rolling. It whacks into the truck, shaking it, and continues down the hill.

If the power-saw operators heard all the screaming about a loose pipe, they would've put their tools down and run for safety. However, required to wear special hardhats with sound-reducing ear guards, they must've not heard, their saws still on.

Cole climbs onto the pipe already in the ditch and leaps out onto the cold, hard ground. His eyes follow the runaway pipe, which is picking up speed. It rushes toward the back of an unsuspecting worker sawing a bracket.

Cole sprints toward him, his hardhat flying off, his arms pumping. He maintains his pace while trying not to slip on the slick, hilly terrain.

The steel pipe decimates the bushes poking out of the snow in its path. If it strikes the worker from behind, the force may sever his spine. Even if he survived the initial impact, it would propel him face-first to the ground, where'd he'd spend the split-second left of his life in pain before the metal crushed his skull.

Cole catches up to the rumbling piece of steel and cuts in front of it, putting himself in its deadly path. He grasps the worker's arm and yanks him toward the end of the pipe.

The man gawks at Cole through safety goggles. He doesn't budge, his circular saw blade still spinning. Cole nods at the pipe. The man's eyes go to it and fill with dread.

He races toward the edge, following Cole. But he's not as fast. The worker had to process so much information in such a short time frame, he's still holding onto his saw, slowing him down. Cole points at the saw and waves his arms in a throwing motion.

The guy seems bewildered for a moment, then understands, heaving the saw over his shoulder mid-stride. The pipe barrels toward him, no more than a yard away. He dives onto the ground face-first, landing near Cole just outside the fatal path.

The tossed saw strikes the top of the pipe. It bounces off and ricochets blade first toward the worker. His face in the snow, he can't see it.

Cole rips off the guy's hardhat. Just before the saw buries itself into the man's back, Cole smacks it away with the high-density plastic hat. The pipe crashes into a wall of trees and comes to a stop in an eruption of branches, pine needles, and snow.

Cole lies on the ground beside the panting man as the rest of the workers scramble toward them.

3

Cole sits in an OB-GYN doctor's office in his hometown, Timber Ridge, his Carhartt work jacket draped over the back of his chair. His fiancee, Lacey, is on the cushioned examination table, in her waitress uniform from Gold Sparrow Diner, a shade of light blue similar to the color of her eyes.

"Good day on the site, babe?" she asks.

He just nods. He refrains from telling her about the worker's life he saved. Even though she'd approve of what Cole did, she may become worked up knowing he was in a predicament with deadly consequences. The doctor once told them that elevated levels of stress hormones could be bad for the pregnancy.

"An old man who's a regular at the counter, and might be like a little senile, peeked at my belly today and asked if they've been giving the staff free food," she says.

"That wasn't very nice of him."

She smiles. It's a fantastic smile. "No. I was happy." She places her hands on her stomach, a slight bump showing nineteen weeks into the pregnancy. "Soon, it's going to be obvious a baby is on the way. I've missed it. Being pregnant out in town is fun."

"Fun, huh?"

"It's the little things. Like, when you're pushing your cart through the grocery store, you can go as slow as you'd like. And nobody is going to cut in front of you."

"If you're going to have an audience behind you at the store, you should practice your pregnant walk. Make sure it's good."

She climbs off the medical table and sashays around the office. "It's going to be elegant." She flips back her long, straight black hair. "And kind of badass at the same time."

"Some combo."

"Then, in a few months, it's going to inevitably turn into a waddle." She starts waddling. "But when it's just me and you, I'll make it a sexy waddle." She stops in front of him, hums a song, and shakes her butt. He taps his hands on it like he's playing the drums.

"Hello," a female voice says at the door, the doctor, a tall blonde in her forties.

Lacey's gyrating rear comes to an abrupt halt. Blushing, she sidles back onto the exam table. Cole looks down at the floor with a grin.

"A medical FYI, you can't make your second baby until the first comes out," the doctor says.

Everyone chuckles. The doctor makes small talk for a bit, then conducts a routine checkup. Soon, a female ultrasound technician joins them in the room and applies a gel to Lacey's bare stomach. Cole grabs her hand with both of his as they watch a black-and-white screen. The technician runs a wand over Lacey's belly.

A tingly sensation fills Cole's chest when he sees their baby on the monitor. He squeezes Lacey's hand a little tighter.

The doctor studies the screen with a slight squint, then turns to the couple. "Start stocking up on pink."

Cole gazes at the black-and-white image of the small girl. His and Lacey's small girl. He pictures that image a bit bigger, out in the world in a baby carriage. Then a bit bigger than that, playing with toys on the floor of his cabin. Bigger yet, roasting marshmallows, riding a bike, wearing a Halloween costume, whispering a secret during a slumber party, doodling in a sketchbook. Then on the stage at a high-school graduation. College next. Then as a young woman in an office somewhere making her way in a career.

In a moment, his light, happy feeling is replaced by a heaviness. A sense of responsibility, more extreme than any he's had, sets in. He's never been a father before. For that little person on the screen to grow into the best woman she can be, he can't screw up. The doctor and Lacey discuss nutrition and various other topics while Cole stays silent.

"I'd recommend registering for a Lamaze class now," the doctor says. "I know an amazing woman from LA who runs a top-of-the-line center. They just opened a branch in Bozeman. Let me borrow your phone for a sec." She pulls up the brand's Instagram page on Lacey's phone. It has over 100,000 followers. Some of the photos feature pregnant celebrities. "Spots fill up fast. You may end up on a waiting list. But I can call her and see what I can do."

Lacey gazes at the spa-like facilities. "Gorgeous. But I'm not really sure if something like this is in our budget."

"True, it's not cheap. A pack of six classes goes for about seventeen hundred. But it's the best in Gallatin County, by far."

Lacey glances at Cole. Almost two grand on Lamaze classes isn't quite doable on his construction-worker income. But if he wants the best for his daughter, he shouldn't get off to a bad start by skimping.

"Give your friend a call," Cole says to the doctor. "We can make it work."

Lacey purses her lips and dips her head, as if to ask, *You sure?*

He realizes he shouldn't mislead his fiancee about money.

Financial deceit has poisoned many marriages. But he sticks with his choice, smiling, as if to say, *It'll be fine.*

His phone vibrates. A text from Ollie. Cole is reminded of the mysterious, hacked-up rabbit at the jobsite. He hasn't told Lacey about that either. A lover of animals, her stress would spike.

Ollie's text: *I have something important to give you.*

4

Lacey's son Declan grunts as he completes another pull-up. Cole stands beside him, holding up nine fingers, counting the reps.

After the engagement, Cole invited Lacey and her son to move into his cabin. She had the boy young, during a previous relationship. Now Declan is twelve, Lacey just thirty-one. Cole installed a pull-up bar in Declan's bedroom and has been teaching him to work out. Getting him into exercise young could form good habits.

Declan does a tenth pull-up, then an eleventh, and goes on to fifteen before letting go of the bar in exhaustion.

"You're a beast," Cole says.

Declan huffs. "Hey, can I ask you something?"

Cole nods.

"There's this eighth-grader at school who's been...weird to me," Declan says. "I didn't want to tell my mom about it. She'd get upset, and maybe call his mom and make it worse."

"Weird how?"

"I think he has a crush on this girl Haylie in my grade. And she, well, I dunno, but I think she likes me, definitely not him.

She always comes to my locker to talk. He says stupid stuff to me, like that my eyelashes, I guess 'cause they're long maybe, that they look like a doll's. He's bigger than me, but now that I've been working out, I think I maybe can win in a fight. But I don't know how to throw a punch. I do, but like not the right way. Is that something you can show me?"

Cole rubs his own neck. "You want to just go up to him and sock him?"

"I don't know. I think, right?"

"No, you don't want to do that. Instead, the next time he says something mean to you, look him in the eye and tell him to stop. Firm voice. Don't look away. See if that works. If it doesn't, we'll go over some other options."

The doorbell rings.

"Let me talk to this man from work for a little and I'll be back up," Cole says, then heads downstairs.

Lacey is curled up under a blanket on the couch with a psychology textbook. Enrolled in online classes, she hopes to become a therapist one day. She sips an herbal tea the doctor said was good for pregnant women.

The flames in the fireplace cast a glow on her and the decorative Chipogee tribal emblem on the wall. After their biological parents died in a car accident, Cole and his brother were adopted by Native Americans, a former carpenter in the family's construction company and his wife.

Cole opens the front door. Ollie stands on the stoop, flecks of snow in his hair and on his hooked nose. Behind him is the whitened front lawn, and beyond that, the whitened peaks of gigantic mountains, faint yet discernible in the rural, night-time darkness.

"Here you go," Ollie says, extending to Cole a thick piece of paper. Across the top, in fancy gold lettering against black, is *You're*

Cordially Invited to the Stallos Energy Annual Gala. "Most corporations do things like this around the holidays. Stallos likes doing theirs at the start of the year. Make it about looking forward, not back. Anyway, the CEO personally told me to give you that. With the weekend coming up, I figured I'd drop it off in person tonight instead of waiting till Monday. Give you enough time to get a tux."

Cole waves the invitation around. "I didn't know a piece of paper could weigh as much as a cinder block."

"You think the invitation is nice, wait till you see what they got lined up for the party. They rented out the Alpine Grand in Bozeman. Five-star resort. Apparently, some king stayed there over the summer. He was from one of those small countries, but still."

Lacey appears at Cole's side. "Hi," she says to Ollie. "I'm the fiancee. Lacey."

"Oliver, but everyone calls me Ollie. Pleasure."

She smiles and drifts back to the couch.

After she's out of earshot, he says to Cole, "Beautiful woman. Good for you."

Cole points at the wedding band on Ollie's finger. "How long's it been for you?"

Ollie lets out a soft whistle. "Going on thirty. She's a beautiful woman, too...in her own way." He looks down at his snowy shoes for a moment. "The party, you in?"

"I'm just an outsourced field contractor. Why am I invited to a corporate gala? The CEO was involved?"

"Word got back to headquarters how you rescued Henzel from getting flattened like an ant today by that pipe. That was some impressive shit, by the way. I checked out your personnel file. I had no idea what you did before you got into construction. Do any of the other guys know you used to be a—"

"Those days are over."

"Anyway, the CEO was appreciative of what you did for a coworker. The invite is a way of saying thanks."

Cole leans against the doorframe. "Nice of Stallos to invite me. But Lacey is studying for a big exam. She's not going to be able to come to a party with me in Bozeman next Friday. So it's probably best if—"

"My wife can't make it either. Roll solo, like me."

"I'm going to be honest, I've never been to anything like this. I wouldn't even—"

"I'm going to be honest, too. Energy companies get a lot of undeserved heat as is. The last thing we need is some story breaking about how our construction sites are unsafe. You come to the party. Drink some nice champagne. Eat some lobster. Enjoy the resort amenities. And if some annoying reporter happens to ask you about a loose pipe on a jobsite, maybe you...you know...say you don't really know much about anything like that."

Ah. Now Cole sees what this is. A soft bribe.

"I wasn't planning on publicizing what happened today," he says. "I'm just glad Henzel is all right. No need to waste your pricey champagne on me. Tell the CEO thanks, and not to worry about—"

"Do it for Maddox Construction, then."

Cole raises an eyebrow in curiosity.

"Some of the most powerful, well-connected people in the US energy industry are going to be at this party," Ollie says. "People responsible for billions of dollars' worth of infrastructure spending in Montana. You bring a few business cards. I'll make a few intros, talk about the good work you and that wacky brother of yours do. In a few weeks, if some VP is asked if they know a good construction firm in the Timber Ridge area...guess who pops into their head?"

He has a point. With the baby coming, Cole needs to fortify

his savings. Even if this party leads to just one small gig, it can be worth a night of his time.

"Speaking of the corporate office," Cole says, "they find out anything about the rabbit?"

Ollie bites his lip. "Actually, yes. I was wrong about the environmentalists. Turns out it was just some demented prank. Our legal team heard from a connection in the state police that chopped-up animals have been getting dropped off at random places across Montana. Not specific to the energy industry. Malls. Fast-food joints. Apartment buildings. It's apparently some dare thing that started on the goddamn internet. Troubled teenage kids going for shock value. You believe that?"

"Huh."

"I'm going to put up cameras in the woods around the job. If these deranged pricks show up again, we'll have 'em on tape for the cops." Ollie glances at his watch. "You coming to this party or what?"

"Do I really have to wear a tux?"

5

Wearing a tuxedo, Cole drives under an archway emblazoned *Alpine Grand*. His windshield wipers labor against a snowstorm. The resort's long driveway slopes toward a stylish log fortress shaped like a cross, light from its windows glowing against the night.

Trees, bushes, and boulders scatter the well-landscaped, many-acre property. In the distance are a couple rows of snowmobiles, which the gala attendees can schedule rides on for the morning, and outdoor, bubbling Jacuzzis. Surrounding the grounds is wilderness, no other buildings in sight.

Cole pulls his Jeep up to the main entrance and a fast-footed valet parks it in a lot among far pricier cars, Mercedes, Bentleys, Ferraris. With his overnight bag, Cole checks in at a desk in the lobby. On it is an *AG* logo, for Alpine Grand, with the top of the *A* designed to look like the top of a mountain. At the room's center is a contemporary, six-foot statue of a frontiersman, the facial features distorted.

Some party attendees break from kibitzing with each other to shoot Cole, the construction-worker outsider, looks of unrecognition. The men wear shiny watches, the women sparkling earrings.

FROZEN DREAM

Many guests have tans, odd in Montana in early January. Maybe they're the remaining traces of sunbathing done on New Year's island vacations.

Cole passes the restaurant off the lobby and walks a modern-painting-lined hallway to his room in the south wing. It's the first five-star room he's ever stayed in. It not only has a big TV across from the bed, but another in the bathroom across from the tub. The pillows seem fluffier than those at a normal hotel. He pats them to check. Yep, much fluffier.

He sets his bag and coat on the mattress and texts Lacey to inform her he arrived okay on the stormy roads. She replies with a heart emoji. He asks how the studying is going and she replies with a peanuts emoji. She considers peanuts her brain food, and often eats them when she wants a mental boost. She must be on a difficult topic. He reassures her she'll ace the test, just like the last one.

Ollie is floating around somewhere, as is Henzel, the worker Cole saved last week. Stallos Energy must not want him speaking to any reporters about the pipe incident, either. Other than those two, Cole knows nobody here. But he'll have to change that if he wants to make connections for Maddox Construction.

He leaves his room. Music carries through the corridor. He follows it around a corner to a low-lit game room with a bar and some tables. About two dozen guests sip drinks around a giant chessboard on the floor with giant pieces. Retro arcade machines blink against the mirrored walls, among a pair of shuffleboard tables. The music comes out of an electronic, neon jukebox.

"You the new guy in sales?" a late-twenties man asks. He's a chunky five foot eight, with boyish dimples. He has a slight lisp, pronouncing the *s* in *sales* with a mild *th*. The impediment sounds like the type that could've been much worse in childhood, and now is ninety percent under control after years of speech therapy.

"Construction worker, actually," Cole says.

19

The kid laughs. When Cole doesn't, the kid's expression makes an awkward recalibration back to serious. "Cool. Very cool. Construction. Nice." He swigs his drink.

Cole can't help but grin. "You a salesman?"

"Compliance manager. But I'm not going to be in compliance forever."

"That so?"

"Tech. That's my calling."

"You into programming?"

"That shit's boring, dude. I can find an army of nerds to do all that for me. I'm talking the business side of the game. The whole economy is getting digitized. Innovation. Industry disruption. I'm trying to be the guy who sees the full landscape." The kid extends his hand. "Sammy."

Cole shakes it. "Cole."

Sammy eyes Cole's tall, fit build. "I got to get back into it. Working out. I was pretty consistent with hitting the gym at school. But after college, with the job, it's been tough."

"You got a sturdy frame, man. You look good."

He gives Cole an appreciative nod. Despite his youth, Sammy has a bald spot. He seems to have gotten quite creative trying to cover it up, his hair loaded with gel, strands pulled across the bare patch like bridges.

"Look, I'll be blunt," Sammy says. "I can use a wingman. These old guys I work with got no game. You seem like you do." He gives a subtle point with his thumb to two pretty blondes by the bar. "I've been playing the long strategy with the one on the left. Little bit later, after this jam starts popping, I'm swooping in."

"Like an eagle, huh?" Cole says, with sarcasm.

Sammy doesn't seem to register the sarcasm. "Yeah, exactly."

"That's not a bad nickname, you know."

Sammy smiles. "Yeah...I can be down with that. 'Bout the chicks, you go for the one on the right. We'll be a team."

"I'm taken, Eagle. Baby on the way."

"Ah snap...all right. Maybe you can at least talk to the one on the right for me? Distract her during my swoop? I've got a lot of content planned. A story about me rescuing a wounded chipmunk, which is only semi-made up. A couple jokes, edgy, but not explicit and, you know, weird. For maximum effectiveness, you'll need to keep the friend occupied for a good twenty minutes, maybe thirty. Think you can help a homie out?"

"The girl on the left, who you like, what's her name?"

"Breann."

"I've got a better idea. Why don't you just walk up to Breann and ask her to lunch?"

"You nuts? That can't be the first thing I ever say to her."

"I thought you've been flirting with her?"

"Subtle glances around the office. Long strategy, remember? Sort of like in the beginning of a Hallmark movie. It hasn't progressed to a verbalization level yet."

Cole rubs the bridge of his nose. "Drop the pre-canned material. Go over there, say hi, and see how it goes. If she seems interested, ask her to lunch."

Eagle gazes at Breann. He is sweating. "Let me, uh, maybe in a sec." He gulps his drink. "By the way, I can hook up your baby."

"Excuse me?"

"Preschool. My dad's best friend is into institutional education investing. He owns the best private preschool in the state, right here in Bozeman. Waitlist is bonkers. I'll put in a call for you, though."

That seventeen hundred for Lamaze hurt. The skin of Cole's back chills when he tries to imagine what tuition at Montana's top private preschool goes for, might be ten times that. After moving in together, he and Lacey couldn't keep their hands off each other, and the baby came as a pleasant surprise. But the on-the-spot financial planning has been far from pleasant. Even if he gets a couple good construction gigs out of this party, they won't be enough to cover a top-tier private preschool, then elementary school, then middle, then high, then college.

Though he never went to college, he would like to see his daughter go. But he can't keep lying to Lacey about what he can afford. Maybe he'll get a second job, work a night shift somewhere. He'd be doing sixteen-hour days, away from his family most waking moments, which is a dismal thought. But that might be what's needed to get his daughter a first-class education.

"Thanks," Cole says. "I'll think about it and let you know."

Eagle leads him to the bar, where Cole grabs a beer. Eagle introduces him to a few coworkers, all older. Eagle takes on a tone of deference around them, as if acknowledging his lower rung in the corporate hierarchy. A silver-haired man shakes Cole's hand and says he's an executive in the firm's legal division.

"Thanks for looking into that rabbit on the jobsite last week," Cole says. "As off-putting as that was, the guys calmed down after hearing they weren't in any danger."

"Rabbit, did you say?" the executive asks. "Like, hop hop, the animal?"

Cole nods.

Puzzlement streaks the man's face. "We did what with a rabbit?"

"Maybe it was someone else in the legal department."

"I'm copied on all major departmental correspondence. And I sit in on an end-of-week meeting with all the managers, which we just had today. I am certain that nobody on the Stallos legal team recently handled anything involving a rabbit."

6

The Stallos corporation's CEO, Rose Stallos, converses with one of her vice presidents in the Alpine Grand's ballroom, in the north wing. Rose wears a sequined Versace gown that hugs her body, which still looks good at sixty-four on a regimen of Pilates and plastic surgery.

The cream-colored walls of the ballroom are covered in a pattern of X-shaped planks, with mirrors in between. A massive chandelier is suspended from the center of the high ceiling on trendy black chains, with smaller globe lamps spread throughout in symmetry. The plush red curtains of the tall windows are pulled back, snowflakes floating outside them.

About a hundred people are gathered in the room, about half standing, the rest at tables topped with bouquets and plates for the soon-to-start dinner service. The help buzzes about refilling champagne glasses, while a trio of musicians produces jazz from a corner.

Through the crowd, Rose spots Ollie. He seems to have come to this party without his wife for the second year in a row. He makes eye contact with her and gives her a thumbs-up, as if to suggest her gala is going well. She lifts her glass in gratitude.

"And this is none other than our fearless leader," says the company's chief financial officer. Rose estimates he's already five whiskeys in. With him is a woman half his age, who must be his new wife, his third. He introduces the two ladies. The twentysomething one has a slight accent, something European.

"You make a beautiful couple," Rose says. "Congratulations."

"Speaking of marriage," the CFO says, "did I ever tell you Rose was married to the company's founder?"

His wife, biting a martini olive off a pick, shakes her head.

"He was a brilliant man," he says. "Built the company from the ground up, a self-made billionaire. He was responsible for bringing Rose into the industry. What was it you did beforehand? I always forget the exact job title."

This prick. He knows what she used to do. Her heart thuds, yet she keeps her smile. "A catalog model."

"Yes, catalog. Isn't that something?"

Rose hopes he drifts away, but he stays planted.

"After the modeling career ended," he says, "as they all inevitably do, her husband got her a job in the Stallos PR department. And she climbed up through the ranks...just like that. Look at her now. CEO."

Before Rose's much-older husband passed away, from cancer two years ago, various names were in contention to succeed him as CEO. The CFO was one. However, on his deathbed, her husband convinced the board to give Rose a try, much to the irritation of the other executives on the shortlist.

She didn't break into this business because she went to a school like Harvard or Princeton, like all of them. She didn't go to any college. The CFO and his ilk never respected her. But she can do this job. Which is why the board has kept her around. She doesn't need to resort to passive-aggressive cocktail-party insults to stick it to the CFO. Stallos's soaring stock price does that for her every day.

"I have to say hello to a lot more people," Rose says, still smiling. "Have a lovely evening, you two."

Her pulse calms as she slips away from him. Brett O'Shea waves to her, a mid-thirties manager in the geosciences division with black hair buzzed tight on the sides. Unlike the CFO, Rose likes Brett. He's not only smart, but a pleasure to be around. A standout lacrosse player in college, he still has a strapping build. He introduces Rose to his wife, who seems just as nice as him.

"You look stunning tonight," the bubbly brunette says to Rose, who bows her head in thanks.

"As do you, dear."

"I landed one a bit out of my league, huh?" Brett says, putting his arm around his wife.

"Oh, stop," Rose replies. "He's quite the catch, too," she says to the young woman. "What he's been doing for us with core analysis is downright brilliant. You should be very proud of him."

Brett's wife gives him a tap on the lips with her finger, which must be some private sign of affection between the couple. While the three talk, Rose notices a strange figure roaming the room. A muscular, six-foot-three man in a black shirt, vest, pants, and gloves. A white covering is over his head with a hole for his mouth, like a ski mask, with black sunglasses over his eyes.

He strolls with his hands together behind his back, nodding at various guests. They smile. They must think he's hired entertainment, maybe a mime, about to perform. However, Rose signed off on every expense for the gala, and something like this was not included.

The man stops at the center of the room. More guests notice him. He stands on a table. A marketing executive applauds, as if watching the start of some zany entertainment act. A few people glance at Rose, as if for a reaction. She must appear worried because unease fills their faces.

The man on the table begins dancing to the band's music. Dirt flakes off his big, black boots, staining the pristine, white tablecloth. Observers whisper to each other. Some shrug in confusion. The dancing man shakes his hips. He steps on a glass, shattering it. A few shards fly onto the rug. A nearby woman gasps.

"Should I take care of this, ma'am?" a voice asks in Rose's ear. The burly resort security guard who's been in the room is at her side.

She nods. He maneuvers through the crowd to the table and says, "Get down, pal. Show's over."

The dancer doesn't stop. The guard reaches up to grab the guy's wrist. The dancer takes a step back, then kicks the guard's face. People scream as the guard totters backward and falls to the floor.

The dancer snatches something from the table, then hops off it and moves his hands to the guard's face. The guard screams louder than anyone else. Rose notices what the dancer took off the table, a butter knife, which he's forcing into the guard's left eyeball.

7

Blood oozes down the guard's cheek. Inside his left eye socket is mush, no resemblance to an eyeball anymore. The dancer cleans the soaked butter knife with the tablecloth and sets it back where he took it. The band has stopped playing. As if from shock, the party guests have even stopped screaming. The large room is silent besides the guard's whimpers.

Rose breaks the quiet by shouting, "Help, security."

Heads turn to the room's main doors. However, they do not open. No other guards come in to protect them.

"I'd like to report a...some sort of break-in and...attack...a knife, an eye, and...oh God...at the Alpine Grand," a jumpy executive says into his phone. "Send police immediately."

The dancer watches him make the call. In the mouth hole of his mask, a smirk spreads. He doesn't seem worried about the cops.

Brett, the young geosciences manager, looks over the crowd. From a physical standpoint, he appears to be the most capable party guest. He takes a deep breath, as if debating whether to intervene in some way. He must decide to, because he steps toward the dancer.

"Brett, no," Rose calls out.

But Brett keeps walking. The former lacrosse player throws a hard punch. But the dancer bends out of the way. He lets out a loud whistle. The swinging doors at the back of the room burst open.

Men in the same outfits as him run inside, holding pistols. A guy carrying two tosses one to the dancer, who blasts the surveillance camera high on a wall. A man stands in front of the swinging service doors, as if to block any guests or staff from leaving, while a second does the same at the room's main entrance. Two others yank the windows' red curtains closed, while another zip-ties the hands of the downed security guard behind his back. Rose reasons that the vests on these men are for stopping bullets.

Though she is stunned, she has a feeling what all this is about. This last week, she was bracing for some fallout over something she did. She considered canceling the party, but would've faced too many questions from her employees that she wasn't willing to answer with facts. At most, she expected a PR problem. Not this. Her eyes find Ollie's in the crowd. He's pale. He must've inferred what this is all about, too.

Brett, as if surrendering in the presence of all these armed intruders, backs away from them with his hands raised. However, the dancer still watches him. Brett's wife hugs him from behind. Tears smudge her makeup.

The dancer plucks a rose from a vase on a table and struts to Brett. His wife shudders, gripping him tighter. Though Brett stands tall, fear seeps into his expression.

"Get on your knees," the dancer says.

"What?" Brett replies.

The dancer turns to one of his men and nods. The second guy clasps Brett's wife's hair and pries her off her husband. She shrieks, as do several others. The man keeps one hand on her hair, angling her head back, and uses the other to stick the butt of his gun under her chin.

"If I nod again, he'll pull the trigger," the dancer says. "If I were you, I wouldn't upset me right now. I'm going to kindly ask you again. Get on your knees."

A bead of sweat drips down Brett's forehead. He glances at his hysterical wife, takes a deep breath, and sinks to his knees.

"Open your mouth," the dancer says.

"What?"

The dancer looks at his man, as if threatening to nod.

"Fine," Brett blurts. His lips begin trembling. They eke apart.

"Wider."

The quivering lips part some more. The dancer shoves the thorny rose stem into Brett's mouth. He gags. The dancer grabs the back of the promising young manager's head and forces the thick stem in even deeper.

"Good boy," the dancer says.

Brett's gagging noises louden. As do his wife's sobs.

"Now suck on it," the dancer says. "Up and down."

Brett is still for a moment, heavy exhales coming from his nose. Then his head starts bobbing along the stem.

"Not tender enough," the dancer says. "Don't just drag your lips on it, suck it."

As Brett sucks, some masked men chuckle.

The dancer looks at Rose and says, "You really know how to get inside your employees' heads, huh, Rose?"

He knows her name. As she suspected, this is a personal attack. These must've been the men responsible for hanging that chopped-up rabbit on the jobsite. She found the meaning of the symbol on the internet. A second rabbit was hung outside her home that day, something she's told nobody at the company except Ollie.

Some executives peer at her, as if waiting for a reaction to the dancer's comment.

"Leave him alone," is all she can think to say.

The dancer doesn't, pushing on the back of Brett's head even harder. "How can you properly suck without using your tongue? Let me see how sweet of a job you can do."

Brett's cheeks swell from his swishing tongue. The thorns must be slicing it, blood trickling from the corner of his mouth.

The dancer makes him suck on the rose for another minute or so, then shoves him to the floor at his wife's feet. Laughing, the second masked man lets go of her hair. She embraces her husband. But he doesn't react, gazing up at the chandelier with glazed pupils.

The dancer meanders through the crowd. Stallos employees and their dates backpedal in fright.

"Here are your instructions," he announces to the room. "My colleagues will divide you into groups. Each gala attendee is going to perform some steps on their phone, which my colleagues will observe. You are to make an account on the cryptocurrency exchange CryptoLX, purchase twenty-five thousand dollars of Bitcoin, and transfer it to me. I go by the name Gemento. With your prestigious jobs, I know all of you can afford it. Excuses will not be tolerated. Follow those simple steps if you'd like to leave here alive."

8

Eagle checks the time on his phone. "Almost eight. Want to head to the ballroom for dinner?"

Cole nods and sips the last of his beer. Minutes ago, a banging noise echoed outside. It didn't bother the others in the game room, who seemed to think it was just an engine backfire from a snowplow truck. But Cole isn't certain.

As he, Eagle, and ten or so more guests head toward the game room's door, it swings open from the other side. Two large, pistol-toting men in black outfits and white masks storm inside.

"Get the fuck back," one shouts. He and his partner move toward the group in coordination, covering each other's back while assessing the room at three hundred sixty degrees. They seem to have training in two-person CQB, close quarters battle.

"Is this real?" Eagle mumbles.

"Just keep calm," Cole says.

Eagle does not. He clutches the knee fabric of his tuxedo pants and hyperventilates. A couple others do the same.

A woman who's put down three margaritas since Cole's been in here chucks her glass at the front intruder. He ducks, then cracks her across the face with the handle of his gun. She falls into the neon jukebox and slumps to the floor. Her bottom lip is torn apart.

He chuckles. "This ugly bitch just got even uglier."

He unplugs the machine, killing the music. Screams boom against the quiet.

While the second intruder guards the door, the first shouts, "All of you, this way." With the barrel of his gun, he prods people toward the oversized chessboard at the center of the room. They circle it. Pacing among the jumbo game pieces, he explains that he'll shoot each party guest who doesn't transfer twenty-five thousand dollars to a crypto account named Gemento.

"Do as he says," a fiftyish man in glasses and a penguin-tail tux declares in an authoritative tone, as if establishing himself as the hostages' de facto leader. He must be the highest-ranking Stallos employee in the room.

Nobody contests him. They don't seem flustered by the twenty-five-thousand-dollar demand, even the younger ones like Eagle. If you're well-off, that's a small price to pay for your life.

But Cole isn't well-off.

He makes a mental note of the intruders' make and model of gun, how they're holding them, whether they're right-handed or left-handed, their exact heights and close-to-exact weights, and the slopes of their posture. Cole then looks around the room, estimating its length and width, and determining potential objects for cover and concealment. Next, he assesses where people in the crowd stand relative to him and the criminals.

Through a window, he can see the top of the north wing, higher up the mountain than the south. Though the game room's windows lack curtains, the ballroom's don't. They're closed, but weren't before. That noise earlier wasn't an engine backfire. Trouble must be up there, too. The thieves may not be alone.

If Cole made a move on these two, even if he were successful, he might have to face others. With a daughter on the way, that's a big risk. If he dies, she grows up without a father. Lacey would lose her fiance. And though Cole is not Declan's dad, he's been easing into a father-figure role. Another loss for a person Cole cares about.

About fifteen minutes pass. As the party guests complete their crypto transfers, the criminal on collection duty works his way toward Cole. When the man gets there, he points his Sig Sauer P220 at Cole's face and says, "You're up." The guy smells like he's been on a long camping trip, woodsiness mixed with BO.

"I don't mean to cause a hitch in things," Cole says. "But I don't have twenty-five thousand dollars. And my credit card's max is less than that. I can't help you."

"Bullshit," the masked man says. He moves the gun closer to Cole, just a few inches from his eye.

Cole doesn't blink. "If you shoot me, your court case for this is going to get a lot more complicated."

"None of you get out of here unless all of you pay," the criminal yells.

"Whose idea was it anyway, to invite some broke construction worker to our party?" the de facto leader in the penguin tails says. "Christ, I'll just cover this fucking deadbeat." He points a judgmental finger at Cole. "When this commotion is over, you and I will work out a payment plan. I don't care how little you make, you're paying me back. If you don't, my lawyer will hound you the rest of your life."

Though Cole is relieved to get the gun out of his face, he's ashamed this guy had to step in on his financial behalf.

"Very kind of you, Farnes," another Stallos employee says to Cole's financial supporter.

"I just want this nightmare to end so I can get back to my life," Farnes replies.

The masked man laughs. "It won't be that simple. Your

money is only the first thing we want. Next, you're all going to be exposed as crooked."

The Stallos employees glance at each other with confused expressions.

"You know what he's talking about?" Cole whispers to Eagle.

"No idea, dude."

At least one connection has become clear. The criminal mentioned "crooked" and a cut-up rabbit is a symbol for corruption. Stallos Energy must've somehow wronged these guys, or so they feel. They're not just out for money, but revenge, which makes them far more dangerous than simple thieves. Cole had firsthand experience with men like this overseas.

Terrorists.

9

A curly-haired executive who told Cole a funny story at the bar about a half hour ago, hunches forward and vomits on the game room's rug. The terrorist chuckles. He nods at Cole's financial supporter, Farnes, and says, "Let's go, pay up for the mooch."

"Wait," Cole says.

The terrorist looks at him over his shoulder. The pile of puke on the floor begins to stink.

"You've already gotten plenty of payments," Cole says. "I'm sure there's more of you up in the ballroom doing the same thing, collecting a lot more. You're in masks. And gloves, not leaving any prints. If you took off right now, you'd probably get away with this."

"If you don't shut your fucking mouth, you're definitely getting a bullet in it."

"I've seen people sending nine-one-one texts. With the snowstorm, the cops may take a while to get all the way up the mountain, but they're coming. Why linger around and risk getting arrested? I strongly recommend you stop what you're doing and leave." Cole keeps his gaze locked on the terrorist's dark sunglasses.

The man just smiles. He doesn't seem worried that hostages were texting 9-1-1. His calmness is concerning.

Cole rubs his temples. He didn't want things to come to this. But if the threat of the police doesn't deter these guys, they must be adamant about carrying out whatever vision of revenge they've conjured up. In Cole's experience, terrorist visions of revenge tend to be bloody and horrifying. He wanted to stay out of this, but he no longer can let himself.

Step one, get the guy to point his gun again.

"It's obvious why Stallos Energy shafted you," Cole says. "Not leaving while you're still a free man makes you a moron. Morons make easy marks for big corporations."

As expected, the criminal sticks his pistol back in Cole's face.

"No, you're the moron," Farnes shouts. "Shut the hell up before you get us all murdered."

"You going to listen to him?" the terrorist asks Cole. "You going to shut up...or call me a moron again?" He cocks back the hammer of his Sig Sauer.

Cole stares at his own reflection in the man's black lenses for a moment, then grasps the gun barrel. He yanks back the slider. With his other hand, he grabs the back of the weapon, then twists it downward and sideways. The terrorist's wrist bends till his grip breaks and Cole pulls the pistol from him. As the terrorist's head bobs in bewilderment, Cole pistol-whips him, just like he did to that innocent woman, only harder. A tooth flies out of the man's mouth onto the chessboard.

The gala guests observe with stunned expressions. The second terrorist sprints over with his gun drawn. Cole sticks the woozy one in front of himself as a human shield. His head and other vital body parts covered, Cole says, "I've got your buddy's gun jammed into his spine. Drop yours or I make him a quadriplegic."

Cole watches the second terrorist on a mirrored wall. The guy does not lay down his sidearm. Instead, he creeps closer, as if angling for a shot. Once the man is about half a dozen feet away, Cole throws a kick between the other one's legs into an oversized chess piece. It launches into the second terrorist's gun hand, springing it upward.

During his split-second of disorientation, Cole charges at him. The guy lowers his arm, preparing to shoot. But Cole clasps his wrist before he pulls the trigger. He smashes the handle of the other gun into the lateral collateral ligament of the man's outer knee.

The guy sinks, groaning. Cole bashes the top of his skull with the Sig Sauer, knocking him out. The guy lets go of his gun, which slides along the slick chessboard surface.

Cole's hears footsteps among the crowd's heavy breathing. Though still dazed, the first terrorist is functional, dashing toward the loose pistol. With one tap of his trigger, Cole could kill him. But if the gunshot noise carried up to the north wing, the terrorist's associates may come down. Instead, Cole grabs a chess piece, the black bishop, and wings it at the guy's feet. He trips and topples to the floor face-first. The impact knocks the sunglasses off his head.

He squirms toward the available gun, but Cole steps on the back of his neck, pinning him in place. The man grunts.

"Eagle?" Cole says, toward the cowering Stallos employees and their dates.

"Umm. Yeah?"

"I need a favor."

Eagle breaks off from the others with slow steps. He looks at Cole like a starstruck fan would a celebrity.

"Pick up that gun," Cole says.

"On it." Eagle darts to the second pistol.

Cole tears the mask off the terrorist under his foot.

10

Rose listens to the worsening storm howl on the other side of the ballroom curtains. Various hotel employees have been rounded up and confined in here with the Stallos hostages, cooks, clerks, valets, maids. Brett in geosciences still has not spoken since the incident with the flower. But Ollie has been supportive to Rose. He stood by her while the thieves broke everyone into groups and remains at her side.

He pats her lower back and says, "It'll all be over soon."

The dancer, who goes by Gemento, circles the room as the antsy guests transfer money. Giving the other thieves orders, he appears to be the leader. He glances at his phone and smirks. He must be watching the balance in his crypto account climb.

Rose's heartbeat picks up as he moseys toward her. "For a bunch of competitive businesspeople, they're quite subservient," he says.

"None of us wants to stand in your way."

He laughs. Chandelier light stripes the lenses of his sunglasses. "Now, it's time to progress to a part of the evening even more exciting than the transfer of wealth."

"You've made millions. What more do you want from us?"

"I need you to call your friend Grant Hampton and advise him to join us here."

"I can't do that."

"Of course you can. Just pick up your phone and ask for a favor. You've asked him for a favor before, haven't you, Rose?"

She looks down at a chipped champagne glass on the rug for a moment. "You want me to convince the governor of Montana to drive a hundred miles from Helena in a blizzard? And then walk into a building taken over by masked lunatics with guns?"

"Lunatics, that's what you think of—"

"No, sorry...I meant...I—"

"No, no. I suppose that's a fair assessment of my colleagues and me, given your limited perspective. But once your perspective broadens, and it will, you will learn that we are perfectly clearsighted."

"Hampton is stubborn. He's not going to take a risk like this."

"Funny. I have a feeling you've convinced him to take an even bigger risk."

This guy seems to know even more than she thought. But she doubts he has any concrete proof. If he did, he would've already gone to the media with it.

"I don't know what you're talking about," she lies.

"You're a good bullshitter, Rose. I'm sure that helps in business. But it's not going to help you now. Or your people. If you can't get Grant Hampton here by midnight, I am going to shoot one of your employees in the face."

Though she tries to keep a steely demeanor, her hand shakes. Gemento stares at it. "If you have a problem with me, let's keep this between us," she says. "My employees have not objected to paying you. They've done enough. Killing one if—"

"You're right. This likely is your fault more than theirs. If you regret getting them into this, the least you could do is get them out. To do that, just get the governor here." He turns around, pulling the walkie-talkie off his tactical belt.

Ollie leans to her and whispers, "Do you think that's—"

"Yes. I've never seen him in person, so can't compare the body type, but who else could it be?" Gemento is, of course, a code name. She suspects she knows his real name.

Ollie looks over his shoulder, as if to assure nobody else is close enough to hear, then says, "We didn't make any mistakes."

"Still, he must've had an idea what happened. Even if he never found any evidence."

Ollie dips his graying head and rubs the bridge of his hooked nose. He doesn't debate her.

"How're things progressing in the south wing?" Gemento asks into his walkie-talkie.

No response on the other end.

After ten seconds or so, Gemento asks, "You there?"

Still, no reply. He paces to another masked man, out of earshot, and they converse. The other guy says something into his walkie-talkie. He holds it by his ear, waiting. No reaction, no reply.

Ollie smiles.

"What the hell could you possibly be smiling about?" Rose asks.

"I don't see him in here."

"Who?"

"That construction worker I told you about. Cole Maddox."

Once the dead rabbits arrived, Rose braced for some leak in the press about what she and Ollie did. Combating the truth with misinformation would've been difficult, though doable. If a second negative story about Stallos broke, a corroborated one about a jobsite pipe almost crushing a worker, the PR department would've been overloaded, susceptible to a mistake. Rose figured a night of free booze would be enough to earn the allegiance of a couple blue-collar guys, and insisted Ollie get them here.

"I don't remember the workers' names," she says. "Clint? What about him?"

"Cole. I counted heads. At least twenty of us aren't in here. Before, I know some others were at a bar in the south wing. They must still be there." He points at Gemento. "Whoever he put in charge down there isn't answering his radio."

"I don't see what that has to do with some construction worker."

"He's not just a construction worker. According to his personnel file, he was a decorated soldier."

"Are you saying he...did something?"

"I've got a friend in Timber Ridge, where he's from. I brought up the name Cole Maddox after the pipe thing. My buddy knew of him, all right. It's hard to tell what's a rumor and what's real. But even if just some of it is true, then yeah, I'd say it's possible he did something."

"I doubt he brought a gun to the party. He'd be outmatched."

"Eh. Ever hear of Delta Force?"

She shakes her head.

"That's by design, I suppose," he says. "The government still doesn't admit it's even real. Most people have no clue it's out there. But you've heard of Army Rangers and Green Berets, right?"

She nods.

"Only the best of the best Rangers and Berets get called up to Delta," he says. "It's the US Army's top unit. These guys get dropped off in the darkest corners of the planet to neutralize America's most sensitive national security threats. The public isn't told about these missions. But without them, we'd all be fucked."

"And this construction worker was one of them?"

"And tonight, he's one of us."

11

Cole gazes down at a shuffleboard table in the game room. The numbers on it are written in the font used on a tee shirt his biological dad used to wear in the spring and summer when he'd work out in the backyard. The sleeveless shirt said *Nat's Auto Repair*. Cole and his brother Jay, both young at the time, would watch him from the window as he lifted dumbbells in the sun, talking about the day when they'd be old enough to try themselves.

A zip-tie is around both subdued terrorists' ankles, another the wrists, while another extends from that around the leg of the shuffleboard table. The unmasked men are about Cole's age, both White. After taking the zip-ties from their tactical belts, Cole patted them down for additional weapons, pulling a pocketknife from one's boot. He snapped photos of their faces and emailed them to the Bozeman Police Department. They're working on identification, plus getting cops here ASAP.

The terrorist who was out cold has regained consciousness, humming a song while the other bobs his head to the tune. Despite their setbacks, they still have a cocky aura, as if this will all somehow work out for them.

"Yo," Eagle says. "Out there in the lawn, is that...a guy?"

Cole walks over, Stallos employees and their dates clearing a path for him. Farnes sits on the floor off in the corner, his penguin tails crumpled beneath him, while his wife helps him get through what appears to be a panic attack.

Since Cole took out the two terrorists, the hostages in the room have come to view him as their leader, asking him various questions. Many wanted to exit the building through the nearby hallway door and sprint down the resort's driveway, off the property. But Cole advised them otherwise. And they listened.

The zip-tied terrorists' walkie-talkies have been going off. Their lack of response is sure to trigger suspicion from their colleagues in the north wing, who are sure to be watching the south wing for signs of irregularity. Anybody spotted outside fleeing would draw hostile attention. The best course of action is to hunker down and wait for the cops to arrive.

Cole looks out the window. The chaotic snow limits visibility, yet a shape the size of a human is noticeable, near a grove of trees. After a long stillness, the shape moves. A man lies face down on the ground, his arms stretched in front of him. His hands appear to be bound to the base of a tree. He wears a black tee shirt with gold lettering. Cole saw a similar shirt earlier, on someone in the lobby.

"A security guard," Cole says. Before making their move on the party guests, the terrorists must've incapacitated the guards on duty.

"Why the hell is he outside in a tee shirt?" Eagle asks.

"His post must've been indoors. They must've lured him out there so they could take him down without anyone inside seeing or hearing."

Cole surveys the surrounding lawn. No other people are out there. Yet, he does notice something near an exterior wall. Black paint stripes some icicles hanging off a gutter. Just below them is a surveillance camera. The terrorists must've spray-painted its lens.

They could've come to the resort in the recent past posing as customers, making note of security cameras, guard posts, architectural details, and more. These aren't hotheads. They're planners. And their plan could have many pieces Cole is still unaware of.

"It's got to be what, negative five degrees out there?" Eagle says. "He's going to freeze to death, man."

Cole is surprised the guard is not already dead. In war, killing an enemy combatant is often easier than restraining a living one. Cole glances at the two terrorists tied to the shuffleboard table. These men had the chance to murder a guard, but spared him, which was a gamble. They may be slimy, but have a moral compass, at least to a degree.

"At that temp, with the high level of wind, he likely has hypothermia by now," Cole says. "If he were in water, I'd take the risk of being spotted outside to cut him loose. But in air, he could survive longer, hopefully until the cops show up. He's probably in a lot of pain, though. I've been there."

"On a construction site?"

"No."

The security guard jerks his arms, as if trying to break free from his binds, with no success. His whole life, Cole's had a powerful protective instinct, which led him to choose a career as a soldier. He wants to go out there and bring the guy into the warmth, but fights off the urge as the man squirms in agony.

12

Rose paces in a corner of the ballroom, out of hearing range from everyone, with her ringing phone to her face. The bands' abandoned guitar, saxophone, and bass are heaped nearby.

"Rose," Governor Hampton says, over the phone. "Tell me you're a yes for our Alzheimer's awareness thing. VIP RSVPs have been a touch low. I get the appeal of the Caribbean this time of year, but how many days in a row can you really pretend to enjoy that tinny Third World music?"

"I got the invitation. It's for Parkinson's, actually."

"That's right."

"Well, I'm, uh, I'm not calling about that. Are you alone on the line? Your assistant isn't listening in, is she?"

"No. Everything all right?"

"Did you guys happen to find a hanging rabbit at the Governor's Mansion a week ago?"

Hampton is silent for a while. "How did you know about that?"

"Do you know what it symbolizes?"

"Someone on my staff mentioned something. I'm a politician. Half the state is going to think I'm corrupt regardless of what I do. We disposed of it and carried on with our day. Why would you—"

"What we did to get the pipeline built. It looks like it may have come back to bite us."

He's again quiet for a bit. "Were our calls, back then, being recorded by someone?"

"It seems there's no hard evidence. But—"

"Then no legal recourse. You sound nervous, Rose. It's unlike you. How is this even a problem?"

"I know he doesn't have any legal recourse. So he opted for a different type of recourse. The gun kind."

Hampton chuckles. "Who convinced you to do this? Cunningham?"

"Nobody briefed you about it yet? Like some police commissioner or somebody like that?"

"I've been at a dinner. You're being serious? He did what with a gun?"

"My entire management team, their spouses, and me are being held hostage at the Alpine Grand. Our...captors...want you to come here and follow their instructions."

"Instructions to do what?"

"They didn't go into detail."

Again, silence. She knows him. She knows he's going to say no. Unlike her, Grant Hampton couldn't give a damn if some Stallos employee died tonight. He doesn't view people as humans, but rather, as levers to pull to advance his political career, her included.

"You have my full commitment this will be resolved in a prompt fashion," he says, sounding like a politician at a podium. "The moment I get off the phone with you, I'm going to personally call the Chief of the Bozeman Police Department. I'll pledge unlimited resources from the state. But...as for me...physically, you know, going there, I just...I really don't see how the angles of that play out to anyone's advantage."

Forty-five-year-old Hampton comes from a long line of timber wealth. His father was a US Senator, and he has ambitions to ascend even higher. Though he's no genius, he has a head of hair like a Ralph Lauren model and a voice like a radio DJ. He looks and sounds good while reading speeches other people wrote, pretending to care about what he's saying. It's his only political asset, yet it's proven effective enough to get him into the Governor's Mansion for two terms. However, if a man is all image and no substance, a single hit to his image can topple him.

"They're going to livestream a hostage killing if you don't show," Rose says. "Sick crap like that goes viral. Millions of people will be watching. Before they pull the trigger, they're going to say something to the camera. They demanded I tell you. They're going to say...this death is due to the cowardice of Grant Hampton."

She's exaggerating. Gemento did mention something about a livestream, though Rose made up the part about "the cowardice of Grant Hampton." She isn't afraid to tell a white lie to keep her employees alive.

"Hmm," is all he says.

Channeling her years in the Stallos PR department, she replies, "If the headline becomes about a dead hostage and a cowardly governor who didn't show up, no way you're going to win the race for the next office you run for. Now, if you're smart, and I know you are, this crisis doesn't have to be a disadvantage. You can spin it into an advantage. A big one, actually."

"How?"

"You livestream your own video. Record yourself on the ride over. Tell the people of Montana...not just Montana, of America...exactly what you're doing. That citizens are in danger. Their governor was called upon. And instead of hiding, he's bravely confronting the armed aggressors. All of America will watch you venture through a snowstorm to help your people in need. You'll look more presidential than Abraham fucking Lincoln."

"That is...fascinating. Let me run it by my people." He hangs up.

She takes a deep breath and stares at herself in a mirror on the wall. Sweat seeps through her makeup in spots, but altogether, she doesn't look terrible. For her employees to remain calm, she needs to continue exuding composure. With a forced smile, she walks to Gemento, giving the hostages she passes little hand waves, as if to say everything will be all right, even though she's far from certain of that.

"Well?" Gemento asks her.

"He didn't definitively say yes yet, but I'm almost positive he'll be here."

Gemento nods, then turns to the masked man beside him and says, "Still nothing from our two in the south wing. I'm going to need you to go down there and make sure everything is okay."

13

The thirtyish woman who was pistol-whipped in the game room peers at her reflection in a mirrored wall. Her cheek is bruised and swollen. Dry blood from her lip, which she doesn't bother to clean up, splotches the parts of her breasts exposed in her gown.

Nobody has bothered to clean up the reeking pile of puke, either. Based on a new odor, at least one hostage appears to have urinated in his or her outfit, no bathroom in here. Stallos employees and their dates have cracked into the room's liquor supply. The bartender, who's broken into a nervous rash, isn't mixing drinks. People swig straight from bottles.

Cole, wanting to keep a clear head, doesn't partake. Neither does Eagle, who has embraced his role as Cole's right-hand man. Together, with a couple other volunteers, they just barricaded the game room's entrance with a shuffleboard table and a few arcade machines. With Cole's guidance, they wedged them in a line between the inward-opening door and a floor-to-ceiling beam.

Cole's phone rings, a 406 number he doesn't recognize. "Hello?" he says into it.

"Hi Cole," a female says. "My name is Shauna Washington.

I'm with the Bozeman PD's SRT, Special Response Team. A road closure from the storm slowed down our patrol units, but they should arrive at the Alpine Grand any minute. I'm en route, not far behind. Once I get to the scene, I'll be serving as the crisis negotiator. An ally on the inside, especially one with a military background like yourself, can be very valuable to someone like me."

"Happy to do whatever I can. Anything on the facial rec?"

"We unfortunately weren't able to ID either man."

"Driver's license photos in the DMV database can—"

"We tried that. The system couldn't find a match with any license picture. Same with mugshots. For that to have happened with one man would be peculiar. For both is...I can't explain it."

"No new information from here either. I've been trying to get them to talk. Whoever put them up to this, they're extremely loyal to."

"But," she says, with some enthusiasm, "our image-match software did get a hit on a recent picture posted to a social-media site. One of the men was at a bonfire party. He didn't post the photo, but was tagged in it. On his own account, he uploads a fair amount of memes, but no photos of himself. The shot looked candid. He may not even know it's online."

"You didn't get his name from his profile?"

"He didn't use his real name, just a screenname. But we were able to pull a report on the account's recent activity. It's liked a lot of posts from another account, called the Children of the Sun."

"Children of the Sun? Never heard of it."

"Neither did I. After we put it out over our network, we got a ping back. From the FBI."

"A domestic terror group."

"The Children of the Sun never committed any crimes, nor seemed to be plotting any, at least publicly. The FBI did not have them classified as a terrorist organization. However, the feds had still been monitoring them."

"For what, violent rhetoric?"

"Yes and no. The group recruits members online with rhetoric that never advocates violence, yet crosses over with a lot of the points made by anti-government organizations that do advocate violence."

"Could be deliberate."

"Yes. The FBI says the language is some of the most sophisticated they've seen in years. It never states anything illegal, while remaining highly controversial and persuasive to the target recipient. The leader seems to be some kind of warped visionary. But just because they never publicly posted anything about violence, doesn't mean they'd hesitate to use it. Our guess is they're behind this situation at the hotel."

"What message are they trying to push?"

"From what I understand, the Children of the Sun's core ethos is that America used to be an admirable country. But since the end of the Second World War, it no longer functions as a republic. Rather, it's become something like a multinational corporation. A handful of powerful families are the shareholders, who reap all the profits and fund the campaigns of politicians. Government's role in this arrangement is to keep the power structure in place, not enact change to benefit the voter."

Cole processes all this for a moment. "Does the FBI have anything on these guys we can use to our advantage?"

"Sadly, no. Though the group has made some waves online, there aren't many official members. The feds estimate a bit over two dozen, tops. It's not big enough to have commanded the resources for a full-fledged FBI probe."

"If the Children of the Sun are so persuasive, why the low numbers?"

"Though their message reaches a lot of people online, recruitment rhetoric suggests they have a physical base. Which now obviously seems to be Montana. Becoming an official member may require you to move and join the others. Like an old-school brotherhood."

"Anything in their posts about why they're after Stallos Energy?"

"The feds are actively digging into the online accounts of assumed members. So far, nothing on Stallos has come up, which is likely by design, to distance themselves from tonight's attack. Just to manage expectations, getting any actionable information will be difficult. These guys all use vague screennames and avoid real photos. Possibly, the FBI can wield an administrative subpoena to get IP address data from certain websites and name some suspects, but that takes time, and in a crisis-situation like the one over there, you don't have much time."

"I unfortunately agree."

"Sit tight, Cole. We'll be there soon."

"So long."

He hangs up. The two Children of the Sun in the room stare at him. They're close enough to have overheard him on the call.

"By the way you fight, I'm guessing you spent time in the army," the one with the missing tooth says.

Cole takes a knee in front of them. "I have some advice for you two. When the cops get here, a crisis negotiator is going to try to get your friends in the ballroom to stand down. If you agree to help her, talk some sense into the others, I bet she'll work out a nice plea deal for you. You haven't killed anybody. You guys can still get out of prison fairly young."

"A lot of your friends get ripped apart by bombs in the Middle East?"

Cole squints at him.

"It's not your fault," the Children of the Sun member says. "And it isn't theirs, either. Patriotism can be a powerful drug. It's blindly led many good young men into the army. It plays on our craving to be part of a group. We've found safety in groups for thousands of years. It's rooted deep in our evolutionary makeup, in every cell of our bodies. But, with all due respect, you chose the wrong group."

"Coming from a man who joined a group of internet weirdos who steal money and pistol-whip innocent women."

"Just a means to a righteous end. We'd be honored to consider a rebel like you for admission. One of our members is a veteran. He's seen the truth. You can too. Were the children of any politicians on the front lines with you in Iraq or Afghanistan? How about the children of any oil executives? That's who you were fighting for. You weren't fighting for freedom, or justice, or democracy, or any other nice-sounding concept they stick in the propaganda. You were fighting for people. Ones who would never fight for you."

Cole stands, peering down at him.

Eagle says, "Yo." His voice is nervous. He points out the window. "Someone else is out there. And he doesn't look like a security guard."

14

Cole looks out the game-room window at a masked man approaching from the east. "Put the booze bottles down," Cole calls out to the room. "Sit on the floor and huddle together. I need you to look more like hostages."

"You heard the man," Eagle yells, clapping. "Take a seat." His speech impediment hasn't surfaced for a while, but does now, the *s* in *seat* with a dash of *th*. As the people sit, Eagle collects their bottles and begins hiding them behind the bar.

The terrorist stops on a hill, facing the game room. Though details are difficult to make out in the blizzard, he seems to lift binoculars to his face. Even with them, no way he can see his two associates tied up on the floor, below the window. If the hostages can sit still, this may not be a problem.

The terrorist gazes this way for a few more seconds. Cole hopes he turns around and heads back to the ballroom. But he doesn't. He slogs through the snowy lawn, as if for a closer look.

If he gets near enough to notice the captured terrorists, he'll panic, calling more down here. Though the Children of the Sun would struggle to get past the barricaded door, they can shoot their way inside through the window. Cole would be forced to take on many of them at once. He's better off dealing with this guy now, one on one, so runs toward the exit.

"Whoa, where're you going?" Eagle asks.

Cole can't waste time explaining. He shoulders an arcade machine out of place, splitting up the wedge between the door and beam, and leaves. He trots through the one-story corridor and opens a door leading to the southwest courtyard, where the terrorist can't see him.

Snow flies into Cole's face. The wind whistles as the bottom of his tuxedo jacket flaps. He sets his foot on the open door's push bar and climbs upward. He grips the top of the wobbling door, then raises himself until getting a foot on it. His slip-on dress shoes don't provide much traction. He reaches higher, to a gutter lined with long, thin icicles, then jumps onto the peaked roof.

The slick, downward slope pulls him toward the ground. But he fights against it, digging his hands through the snow, clutching roof shingles for support. He scrambles up the incline to the roof's ridge and hooks his arms over it for stability.

Without a coat, the cold penetrates his body. He spots the terrorist in the lawn, working his way toward the game-room window. Cole grabs the Sig Sauer tucked in his pants. A gunshot would get the attention of the other Children of the Sun. But Cole could jump off the roof and strike this guy over the head with the pistol.

Keeping low, Cole watches the man approach. As the guy nears striking range, Cole inches over the ridge to the east side of the roof. Though the terrorist doesn't spot him, someone else does. The tied-up security guard.

The terrorist notices the guy gawking and looks the same way. Cole must act now or get shot, so leaps off the roof.

The terrorist takes a rushed step backward. Cole swings the Sig Sauer at him. But the man's head is still a touch far. Cole hits his chest and crashes down on top of him. Cole's hip bangs against the man's knee, pain shooting through his leg. A moment later, Cole's jaw whacks the binoculars, a worse pain consuming his face. Warm blood wells up between his bottom gum and lip.

Cole reaches for the gun in the guy's holster, but the terrorist hops back and gets to it first. Cole clasps his opponent's wrist and yanks his arm outward, moving himself out of the potential line of fire.

The terrorist, who's even bigger and stronger than the two inside, muscles his way to his feet. Cole rises with him and swings the Sig Sauer at his head. The man ducks and grabs Cole's wrist.

They're in a deadlock, each holding the other's gun hand in place with his free hand. The terrorist must've removed his sunglasses to look through the binoculars, his angry, beady eyes exposed in the mask.

Cole tries a kick, but his opponent throws a defensive one into Cole's ankle. The guy tries kicking Cole, who pulls the same defensive move. Cole considers throwing a knee, but the terrorist's long arms have him set too far back for an effective impact.

The man grunts, trying to yank his gun hand away. Cole holds it steady, but won't be able to all night. If he's going to win this fight, he needs to get creative.

He assesses his surroundings, then drives his legs forward, pushing the terrorist into an exterior wall of the hotel. The guy's back slams into the snowy logs. He grits his yellowish teeth and snaps a head-butt. Cole evades a direct hit, yet his ear absorbs a partial blow. It throbs.

Cole drags the hard heel of his slip-on dress shoe against the ground until the back of his foot comes out and flings the shoe upward with his toes. It smashes into the sharp icicles on the gutter. A few break off.

Cole tugs the guy into their path. An icicle cuts the left side of his neck. At just a one-story fall, the slice isn't deep, yet it's enough to cause an involuntary hitch of the terrorist's arm. His grip loosens a bit. Cole rips his own arm counterclockwise, freeing his gun hand. He swings the Sig upward, bashing the bottom of his opponent's chin.

Before the man regains his bearings, Cole hammers the pistol handle into his forehead. The terrorist's eyelids flutter. He staggers for a second, then plops to the ground, unconscious.

Cole catches his breath, coming out of him as vapor in the cold. He spits, his blood dotting the snow, and puts his shoe back on. He pulls a pair of zip-ties off his opponent's belt and secures his ankles and wrists. In the distance, a sound brings relief. A police siren.

Down the hill, between the evergreens along the road, the lights of two police cars flash. If the Children of the Sun in the ballroom don't do the smart thing and give up, a SWAT team will rush in and end this for them the hard way. Either way, it's all about to be over. The first cop cruiser hooks a right onto the Alpine Grand's driveway and starts ascending it.

A boom rises above the sirens. The police car lifts off the ground in a ball of flames.

15

Hostages in the ballroom wince as the sound of the explosion rumbles up the mountain. They look at Gemento and the other masked men for a reaction. They give none.

"What the fuck was that?" a woman blurts. She, like the rest, are unable to see outside through the curtains, which will also stop the cops from seeing in, preventing them from an attempt to take out the Children of the Sun via sniper.

Gemento nudges a curtain to the side, not far enough for anyone to see into the room. Outside, a toppled police car blazes, the glow of the flames illuminating the nearby lawn. The two cops crawled out. One is on fire, thrashing around in the snow.

These two were just doing their jobs. Gemento can't help but feel bad for them. The torched one could have third-degree burns, a face like a melted candle for the rest of his life. However, Gemento doesn't feel that bad for them. They were dumb enough to take a police job.

Now, the rest of the force will be shaken and hesitant. The effect has already materialized. Farther down the hill, a second cop car is parked on a slant, as if it skidded to a stop after the explosion. From his burner phone, Gemento calls the department's general number.

"Bozeman PD," a friendly male voice says.

"Hello. I am not certain if word got back to headquarters quite yet, but one of your patrol cars just ran over an IED at the Alpine Grand. I do not want this to happen to another one of your vehicles. I'm sure you don't either. So, I will give you some instructions to prevent that. All you need to do is relay them to the others in your department. Can you do that for me?"

A long pause. "Yes." The man's voice is no longer friendly. It sounds serious, and a tad scared.

"Terrific. More explosives have been laid on the grounds of the Alpine Grand, not just the driveway, but all over the lawn. Some are even miles away in the forest surrounding the property. These devices are small, flat, and dark. Without the snow, they'd be nearly impossible to see at night. With a snow cover, impossible. If weight above ten pounds is put on them, they will detonate. Please advise your colleagues not to approach the hotel from any direction, so they can avoid a regrettable catastrophe. Understood?"

"Yes."

"Excellent. Any more patrol cars you send are to stay on the road leading up to the resort, at a distance of at least one mile. Same goes for press vehicles and any others that arrive."

"Yes."

"Lovely. If this rule is violated, I will be forced to execute a hostage. Another happening I want to avoid. You as well, I'm assuming?"

"Yes." The fear in the man's voice is even more evident.

"One last message. Once you convey what I've told you to your colleagues, I am almost positive someone who views himself or herself as an outside-the-box thinker will arrive at a certain conclusion. In an excited voice, they will say, 'If we can't get to them by ground, we will by air.' Others will offer this person a pat on the back, then send a helicopter to hover above the hotel and lower a SWAT team onto the building. Please warn the Bozeman PD not to do this."

"Yes."

"I really hope you're not lying to me. My associates and I brought an RPG with us. If we see a helicopter approaching, it will be blown out of the sky with a rocket. Everyone inside will die. This is something else I do not want to happen. You neither?"

"Yes."

"Good. That's all." Gemento hangs up.

In the periphery of his vision is the big chandelier, five tiered rings of crystals. It reminds him a bit of the one in the banquet hall where his wedding reception was held nineteen years ago. The Alpine Grand's is much nicer, but something about the way they glisten is similar.

"Quick update," Hectus says.

Gemento turns to his late-thirties associate. Hectus, a code name, is six feet tall with shoulders as broad as a man's a foot taller. His long-sleeved black shirt stretches over the bulging muscles of his upper body. The shapes of some forearm veins are visible under the form-fitted, athletic fabric.

"Nothing back from anybody in the south wing," Hectus says, in a just-the-facts tone.

"All three of them?"

Hectus nods.

"Whatever is happening in the south wing seems to be turning into a real issue," Gemento says.

"A few of the Stallos people could've banded together and bull-rushed our men."

"Doubtful. Look at the ones up here. They're petrified. They haven't tried a thing. Whatever is happening down there is...different."

Hectus's masked head tilts to the side, in contemplation. "Should I go down there myself and look into it?"

Hectus trained the others for tonight's siege. He spent his late teens and early twenties in the military. A talented soldier, he was on his way to rise to the top of the Special Forces. But after a year in an Iraqi basement as a POW, his situation changed.

He has scars all over his legs, about the size of nickels, from the screw gun the enemy would bury into his thighs while questioning him. The leg holes didn't break his resolve. He didn't give up any intel. But they did disrupt his mobility, preventing him from fighting once US troops freed him. Though full function has since returned to his legs, the injuries derailed his military career.

Like many other vets, he came back home and tried working in the private sector. But he couldn't hold a job. Small confrontations with coworkers or customers would set him off. PTSD, he was told. He never hit anyone, just raised his voice. But that was enough in the modern, too-sensitive, too-soft work environment to make him a monster.

When he called the army for help, he was hoping they'd find him a job from their extensive network of private-sector contractors, pair him with a company that understood his context. But all the army did was give him a 1-800 number for a mental health counselor. She was twenty-seven years old and never served a day in uniform. She told him to get more sleep and drink herbal tea. It didn't work.

"The last two times we sent men down there, they haven't come back," Gemento says. "Though I'm confident you can handle yourself, let's not chance putting you in a predicament unless it's absolutely necessary. I need you by my side to see this night through."

"What about our three guys down there?"

"We already have over two and a half million dollars in crypto, more than enough to buy a big plot of land, put up some housing, and begin our life of freedom in Moldova. And I just heard the governor is on his way. Once he arrives and we finish our business here, we'll kick off the exit procedure. We can completely bypass whatever trouble is going on in the south wing."

"And just leave our three guys behind?"

Gemento, who started the Children of the Sun a year and a half ago, only offers membership to people like Hectus, who've been wronged by the corporate-political system in a life-altering way. Though Gemento cares for all of his disciples, he needs to be sensible.

"This is a mission, something you're more familiar with than anyone else," he says. "Our allegiance must be to the cause, not individuals. If we poke this problem in the south wing, it may get worse. We can't risk our revolution for three men."

Hectus grunts. He does not seem to like this conclusion, yet does not disagree.

16

A third Children of the Sun member is zip-tied to the third leg of the game-room shuffleboard table. After the police car exploded, Cole hauled the unconscious terrorist behind a tree, staying within the man's footprints in the snow in case other bombs were laid on the ground.

With the binoculars, Cole watched the ballroom windows. Sure enough, the curtain over one opened a touch and a guy gazed outside, as if to survey the explosion's aftermath. Once the curtain closed, Cole asked the security guard about his path over the lawn, then uncut his bound hands with the pocketknife he found earlier.

The guard, Diaz, a Latino, is inside in the warmth of the game room. But his problems are far from over. He has a nasty slash across his thigh from the knife of the terrorist who attacked him. Already down a lot of blood, Diaz's thin body shivers on a chair. With his tuxedo jacket, Cole created a tourniquet for the wound. Eagle draped his jacket over him for added heat and got him a bottle of water. The bleeding is somewhat under control, however, if Diaz doesn't get to a hospital within a few hours, his condition could deteriorate. He could lose the leg.

Cole's phone rings. Shauna, the crisis negotiator.

"Any updates?" Cole asks.

"Not good ones." She explains that more pressure-plate IEDs are hidden around the property, like he suspected. That, plus an RPG threat, have thwarted a SWAT raid. According to texted reports from ballroom hostages, many more terrorists are inside the hotel, a dozen total. Complicating matters even more, the governor of Montana has been summoned to the resort for some mysterious reason.

Cole runs a hand through his hair. His ear still throbs from the fight outside. "The Children of the Sun obviously would want to avoid stepping on their own IEDs. There's no way they haphazardly scattered them around the property. There must be a map, with the location of every one, that each of these guys has a copy of."

"If that were me, I'd want to be damn sure where those things were. I'd want something digitized. An interactive GPS map loaded with the lat-long coordinates of each."

"Phones."

"Mm-hmm. Phones."

"Let me see what I can do."

He hangs up. On the shuffleboard table the three terrorists are bound to are items pulled from their pockets, including their phones. Cole checks the first. The only entry method is a PIN. He tries the second. Just a PIN. However, with the third, he sees an option for fingerprint recognition. It belongs to the one with the missing tooth who tried to convince Cole his entire military career was a sham.

Cole whacks the man on the side of the head with his palm, fazing him, then tears the glove off his right hand. Cole jams the groaning guy's thumb onto the screen, unlocking it.

Cole looks at the icons of the apps on the burner phone. Not many are on there, just the type that tend to be pre-installed. The photos app has no saved photos. The text-messaging one has a couple threads, but the content is scant, a few operational questions with terse answers, like:

In position?

Yes.

No sign of a map anywhere. These guys must've been smart enough to know phones are vulnerability points on missions. They could've communicated on different devices while planning, then brought stripped-down ones tonight just to satisfy basic tech needs. As for the IEDs, they must've plotted out where each would go, relying on landmarks and pace counts, and memorized the locations. Cole can't help but be somewhat impressed.

The terrorist must know Cole just tried and failed to cultivate intel off the barren phone. He smirks, showing the bloody gap in his teeth.

Cole texts Shauna, telling her about the brick wall with the terrorists' phones. She texts back:

At this point, let's just sit tight and see what they want with the governor. They've already made a lot of money. If the governor follows their orders, they may chalk this night up as a win and let the hostages go.

Cole has a bad feeling about Governor Hampton entering this environment. The Children of the Sun view themselves as victims of an oppressive corporate-political system run by a well-connected inner circle. Trust-fund-possessing politician Grant Hampton would be the embodiment of that inner circle.

If they have reason to believe he acted alongside Stallos Energy in some corruption scandal, a cruel exaction of retribution may be in store for him. Though Cole isn't a fan of the governor, he doesn't want to see the man maimed or murdered tonight. Cole tries to come up with a plan to stop the terrorists. But the IED and RPG obstacles are difficult to strategize around.

Diaz groans, adjusting his leg. The tux-jacket tourniquet is soaked in so much blood it has the appearance of a candy-apple shell.

"How're you feeling?" Cole asks.

Diaz gulps the bottle of water, finishing it. He shakes his head. His black, shaggy hair, the tips of some strands still icy, sways over his light-brown forehead. With some fine wrinkles, he appears to be in his early forties. "I'm sorry. I'm so sorry."

"For what?"

"This is all my fault."

"What're you talking about?"

"I was dead broke and needed a job to pay the bills. This dumb rent-a-cop gig was the only decent-paying thing I was qualified for. I didn't take it seriously. I smoked a blunt before work tonight." He has tears in his eyes. "I'm a security guard. I was supposed to keep this place secure. And I fucked it up. I fucked it all up."

He dabs a tear. His arms are covered in tattoos. A long-haired woman's face, an ocean wave, a heart with a date inside, a couple phrases in Spanish. Among them is a shield with a *Semper Fi* banner.

"Were you a Marine?" Cole asks.

Diaz nods. "You serve, too?"

Cole nods. "You Marines are tough. Don't let this get to you. You couldn't have prevented what happened on your own. It's not your fault."

Eagle, who must've noticed Diaz finish his water, jogs over with another bottle, his tubby stomach jiggling.

"Hey, thanks man," Diaz says.

"No problem. I'm Eagle, by the way." They shake hands and start talking.

Cole keeps thinking, trying to figure out a plan. He feels an idea developing in the back of his mind, but can't quite see it yet.

17

Shauna, a thirty-seven-year-old, Black single mother, stands under an open-sided tent a bit over a mile east of the Alpine Grand. The cold wind burrows under her Bozeman Police parka. She's in decent shape, but has bad knees. They've started aching, which happens when she's on her feet for long.

Her captain, two FBI agents, four EMTs, four patrol cops, and a six-person SWAT team are with her in the makeshift command center on the closed-down street. The windshields of their parked vehicles are blanketed in snow.

Tonight, Shauna's two kids are with their grandma. Her son tends to be asleep by now. But her daughter, who's a couple years older, thirteen, likes staying up late when at grandma's house. They eat microwave popcorn on the old sofa and watch episodes of reality TV saved on the DVR. Shauna is watching a form of reality TV as well, but isn't enjoying it.

Against the advice of authorities, Governor Hampton decided to announce the hostage ordeal to the public on social media. Sipping coffee from a thermos, Shauna gazes at the livestream on her phone, of him inside a Chevy Tahoe on his way here.

"In times like this, it's important we turn to the values that bring us together," he says into the camera, "not bring us apart."

He wears an American flag pin on the lapel of his two-thousand-dollar suit. His teeth look so white they almost appear neon. Shauna wonders if he put some special dye on them just before recording.

"Compassion," he says. "Keep an open mind about your neighbor, whether rich or poor, White or Black, young or old. It's simple, people. Compassion. That's what makes us Americans strong. Whatever is happening tonight, whatever these individuals want, I assure you it does not come from a place of compassion. And when I arrive, I won't hesitate to tell them that." He points his finger. "I'm going to say this is wrong. This isn't what we stand for in this great republic."

"Do you think the terrorists caught wind he's doing this?" a patrolman asks, watching at Shauna's side.

"Yep."

"I'd imagine they're not going to like it much."

"Nope."

The sound of an engine approaches. A news van.

"Crap," the patrolman mutters. He jogs toward the van, waving his hands to stop it.

Shauna receives a call. Cole. She closes the livestream and asks, "What's up?"

"How far out is Hampton?"

"Under an hour."

"That might be enough time."

"For what?"

"I know you can't fly a chopper over here. But what about something smaller? The size of an eagle. They wouldn't notice that in the storm."

"We're going to stick half a dozen two-hundred-pound SWAT guys on some object just a few feet long?"

"You're going to send them in after. Once you have the intel."

"What intel?"

"Hampton doesn't know where the IEDs are. When he shows up, a terrorist is going to have to come out and walk him up to the hotel. That's why they wanted you guys a mile away, so you couldn't see the safe path they took. If you can fly a drone over Hampton while he's escorted inside, you'll have a clear aerial view of how they take him up the hill. SWAT can retrace the steps."

"Huh. I like it. But there's an issue." She glances out at the storm. "Drones can't fly in the snow."

"Military-grade ones can. I've used them. You with any feds?"

"A couple."

"They can probably get one over here."

Once Hampton arrives, the terrorists may get suspicious if he lingers. If this plan is going to work, the military-grade drone must be here in fifty minutes. She hangs up, not even willing to waste a second to say goodbye, and dashes to the two FBI agents.

18

The Chevy Tahoe transporting Governor Hampton drives along a winding, evergreen-lined road in Bozeman. It trails the police-escort vehicle that's cleared traffic for it since Helena. From a bucket seat in the SUV's second row, Hampton peeks at the console clock. 11:41 PM. Just nineteen more minutes till the arrival deadline.

In the seat next to him is his assistant, an attractive twenty-eight-year-old who's been recording him on her phone. Hampton's phone, in his pocket, has been vibrating quite a bit the last half hour or so. But, fixated on his livestream, he hasn't checked it. This is his moment. Over 200,000 people are watching.

The SUV slows, then stops. Continuing to address the camera, Hampton glances out the windshield. The police car ahead idles. The two cops exit and approach a fallen tree blocking the road, a casualty of the storm. They struggle to move it. The chauffeur opens his door, cold wind gusting into the SUV, and trots over to help.

Once the tree is out of the way, the time is 11:53. The driver hits the gas, yet keeps the vehicle far below top speed on the icy road. Soon, parked law-enforcement cars, ambulances, and news vans come into view. The cops wanted Hampton to stop at the tent for a quick debrief before proceeding to the Alpine Grand, but after the slowdown with the fallen tree, he lacks the time. Still yapping to the camera, he taps the driver on the shoulder and waves his hand, a signal to keep going.

A Black woman in a police parka steps out into the street with her palm up, requesting they halt. Whatever some Affirmative Action hire has to tell him can't be as important as arriving at the hotel on time and avoiding the PR catastrophe of a hostage death. Once again, he waves his hand at the driver, who zooms past her.

Per the instructions of the terrorists, just the vehicle carrying the governor is to get within a mile of the hotel. The police escort pulls over, while the Tahoe winds farther up the mountain. Soon, the lights of the Alpine Grand glint among the snow and darkness.

"Unfortunately, it's come time for me to sign off," Hampton says to the camera. "Though I won't be able to speak to you while I'm inside, you all will be in my thoughts. And in your thoughts, I hope you keep the brave men and women held captive. God bless."

"That's a wrap," his assistant says, an excited lilt to her voice.

He stretches his neck, cramped from turning his head to her for the last two hours. "What sort of sentiment are we seeing on social?"

The SUV stops at the base of the hotel driveway as his assistant scrolls through online comments for trending posts containing #granthampton. She smiles. "Looks like it might not be too early for me to pick out my dress for the White House inauguration."

Hampton reads some of the positive feedback. One of the posts includes a screenshot from the livestream. Though the top comment does refer to him as "handsome," the video filter isn't the one he prefers for low lighting. His assistant should know this by now. He takes a deep breath.

"Everything all right?" she asks.

He restrains himself from snapping at her. Five months ago, in a moment of weakness after four whiskeys at a zoo grand opening, married Hampton let her blow him. Ever since, he's been extra cautious about criticizing her work, fearing she may go public.

"Yes," he says. "Everything's fine. Just, you know, thinking about the people inside."

"I'm sure you'll come up with something to resolve all this. They're lucky to have you as their hero."

At midnight, the silhouette of a man appears in the SUV's headlights.

"God," the assistant says in a jumpy voice, taking in the guy's tactical black outfit, white mask, and rifle. "It's like a scary theme-party costume. But...real."

Though Hampton would take any risk to up his odds in a Presidential race, he sure isn't looking forward to this, his heart thumping at the sight of the terrorist. He puts on his coat and steps out into the blizzard.

The terrorist points down the road, commanding the driver to leave the way he came. Once the SUV disappears into the storm, the terrorist pats down Hampton, finding no weapons, then marches up the hill toward the hotel, a few yards to the side of the driveway.

"Follow me," the man says.

The piled snow soaks the bespoke shoes Hampton bought in London last summer. He passes a charred cop car on its side. He's sure he was notified of the incident in one of the many unread emails that accumulated during the livestream. In the air is a scent reminiscent of barbecue food. It must be from burnt flesh. Gross.

The terrorist grabs Hampton's arm and pulls him on a zigzag pattern up a portion of the lawn, almost like he's avoiding something on the ground. Hampton's neck is still cramped. He rolls his head on his shoulders, trying to loosen up. When his head dips backward, he spots something above him, high in the sky. A machine. It's flying. A drone.

He knows the army uses these things to drop bombs and considers if the terrorists are about to drop one on him. He takes a jerky step back, trying to get out from under it. The terrorist looks up, as if to see what Hampton is staring at.

The guy's upper body stiffens. He aims his rifle at the drone and fires. A loud blast echoes. The drone plummets onto the top of a tree in the lawn and falls to the snow, a couple dozen feet away.

The terrorist stomps over to it and blurts something into his walkie-talkie that Hampton can't make out with the distance. The radio conversation goes on for a couple minutes, then the terrorist clasps Hampton's hair.

"Ahh," the governor screams.

"Nice try."

"Try at what?"

The terrorist yanks Hampton up the hill by his well-conditioned, blow-dried hair, zigzags again, and drags him through the main entrance of the Alpine Grand.

19

Panicky game-room hostages ask Cole if the loud bang they just heard outside was from a gun. Though Cole believes it was, he doesn't say so, trying to keep them at ease. However, that doesn't seem to be working.

Diaz, the security guard, nudges down the tuxedo-jacket tourniquet over his thigh and peeks at his knife wound. He grimaces, covering it back up. "It doesn't look too good, man," he says. Face down outside for a while, his pants slashed, his open wound exposed to the dirt, he may have an infection. "Up the hall, we've got some medical stuff for snowmobile accidents in a supply closet. I think I should clean the cut, get some medicine on it."

"Don't risk going out there quite yet," Cole says. "There're ambulances just down the road. Any minute now, the cops should hopefully know their way around the bombs. Once SWAT takes control of the ballroom, we'll get you over to the hospital."

Cole's phone vibrates. A text from Shauna:

Bad news. The governor, wrapped up in his damn livestream, never got the message we were watching him with a drone. On the feed, we saw him look up at it. He got the attention of the terrorist with him, who shot it down...before we could map the full path up the hill.

Cole's stomach sinks. Yes, that was a gunshot. Though he is glad nobody was murdered, losing the drone was detrimental. The governor's footprints in the snow would mark a safe path up the hill, but now, at least one terrorist must be watching the sky for a second drone, ready to take it down. Even if not, by the time the FBI got another one here, the tracks could be covered by fresh snow. Their best hope to resolve this terrorist takeover failed. Now, no end is in sight.

Cole asks Diaz, "Where exactly is that supply closet?"

Diaz must be able to read the disappointment on his face. "Was that the cops? Everything...decent?"

"We may all be here for a bit longer than we hoped."

Many hostages overhear this. Postures deflate. Heads hang. Diaz stands, shifting his weight to his uninjured leg, the set of keys on his belt jingling.

"Need help?" Cole asks.

"You've done enough for me. I can get to the first-aid kit myself. Stay here with them. They need you." He grabs one of the giant chess pieces, the white king, like a cane.

Cole removes the bulletproof vest from a captured terrorist and hands it to Diaz with the third pistol. "Just in case."

Diaz nods, tosses Eagle back his tux jacket, and staggers toward the exit. Trailing him, Eagle points at the barricade, as if to signal he'll disassemble and reassemble it.

"What are we supposed to do now?" an auburn-haired woman in her mid-forties asks Cole. The sparkle of her diamond earrings contrasts with the dread in her face.

"For now, the best thing we can do is stay calm."

Nobody seems enthused about his answer. He wishes he had a better one. Coming up with a new plan will be even harder to do than the last. After the drone shootdown, the terrorists in the ballroom will be on high alert for another ploy.

"Holy shit," a guy blurts, staring at his phone. His jacket off, deep sweat stains circle the armpits of his white shirt. "Look at this."

People huddle around him, Cole joining. The guy smells like worn socks. On his screen is a livestream of the ballroom. The hostages inside have a similar weariness to the ones in the game room, Ollie among them.

At the center of the frame is a woman Cole recognizes from the financial press, Rose Stallos, the company's CEO, and the governor, at her side. His hair is a mess. A tall terrorist paces in front of them. Shauna described the leader, Gemento, as taller than the rest, six three. This seems to be him.

"How'd you get this?" a woman asks the man holding the phone.

"My son sent it to me. He's been following the story on social media. Someone must've posted this link."

The pacing terrorist says to the camera, "For long enough, hardworking Americans have been taken advantage of. Citizens like us contribute labor to an economy, while businesspeople like Mrs. Stallos reap the bulk of the profits while bypassing any actual risk. Does Mrs. Stallos put on a hardhat in the morning and attach steel pipes in the cold weather? No, she sits in a plush office, counts the money those pipes generate, and puts most in her own pocket, paying those who created the infrastructure just enough to eke out a modest living."

Circling Rose, he continues, "If a worker runs into a challenge, like a bad back, he's laid off. But if a CEO like her runs into a challenge, she can cheat her way around it. It's all rigged, an easy life for those at the top and cutthroat Darwinism for everyone at the middle and bottom. The modern USA is one big scam. The system violates common sense. Yet, it persists. How can people like Mrs. Stallos get away with their behavior?"

He pauses for a couple seconds, then flicks the governor's hair. "Politicians like this let them get away with it. All these people at the top are allied, swapping favors. Governments control our laws, handpicking which are enforced, and on whom. And they control the enforcement mechanism...the cops, the men and women with guns. That's what it all ultimately comes down to, my friends...physical violence. This modern system of ours isn't so modern. It stands on an ancient bedrock principle. Question your masters and get locked up. Resist, get hurt."

His index finger wags a couple times. "Here's the most interesting part. We have more guns than them. In America, civilians possess around four hundred million firearms, while the cops have about a million. We can outgun them four hundred to one. Yet, we do nothing about their tyranny. Why?" He points at his head. "People like Rose Stallos and Grant Hampton know most of us are herd animals. We're scared of being the first rebel. We'll only join a cause once it's picked up numbers. Well, tonight, let me be your first rebel."

He puts one hand on Hampton's shoulder, his other on Rose's. The governor and CEO flinch at his touch, yet maintain composure. "I'd like each of you to look into the camera," the terrorist says, "and tell America what you did to get the new pipeline built."

The camera zooms in on the faces of Hampton and Rose. They make eye contact with each other for a moment, then look away. Rose adjusts her necklace. Hampton bites his lip.

"Like I promised in my last campaign," Hampton says, "I fought hard to get the Stallos pipeline approved to bring thousands of new jobs to the Montana economy. Like all great achievements, the process was not fast nor easy. We had to interface with many leaders from the tribal and environmental communities. After plenty of long hours from my team, and the Stallos team, I'm proud to say we found a mutually beneficial solution. And pipeline construction is currently underway."

The terrorist points his pistol at a nearby woman and shoots her in the face.

20

A lanky woman in the game room shrieks. She backpedals on her purple high heels away from the phone with the livestream and slips on the chessboard, rolling her ankle. Outside, the echo of the ballroom gunshot carries through the mountain air.

"Oh God," a man with a salt-and-pepper beard mutters, his hand over his heart.

"What just happened?" another guy asks, in an antsy voice. He's at the back of the huddle, too far to see the screen.

"They just shot Melinda," the man with the phone says.

The hostages go silent. A few sit, not bothering to find chairs, just sinking to the floor. "Why Melinda?" asks a seated woman with a Japanese-symbol tattoo on her calf.

"She was just...standing there," the guy with the phone says in a hollow tone. "She didn't do anything to provoke it."

The room goes silent again, as if the hostages are absorbing their dire new reality. If Melinda was killed at random, any of them could be, too.

On the screen, Rose has dropped to a knee. Ollie crouches at her side, saying something to her inaudible. Melinda lies on the floor, the top half of her body obscured by a man in a tuxedo hovering over her, performing useless CPR. Her legs stay motionless.

Soon, the livestream cuts off. Some hostages in the game room return to swigging alcohol straight from the bottle. A redheaded lady makes a call, Cole guessing to a family member, and says a teary goodbye, just in case they never see each other again.

"Please, do something," the woman with the calf tattoo says to Cole. "Anything. We can't just stay trapped in here, waiting to die."

Two other women give him similar pleas. Though the men may be embarrassed to ask him for help, many do with their eyes, staring at him like helpless animals in a forest.

"Let's all stay calm, like he told us to," Eagle says to the room. His tux jacket, held by a finger, is slung over his shoulder. He walks to Cole and says in a soft voice, "As your number two, I figured you'd want me to project a sense of cool, hoping it rubbed off on the others." He nods at the jacket over his shoulder. "You like this move, sort of like a Dean Martin thing?"

"That's some move."

"Though I may look cool, between you and me, I'm not feeling too relaxed about things. In fact, I'm scared shitless. Please tell me you have an idea."

"Let me touch base with the cops."

"I'll dole out waters. Keep 'em hydrated."

Cole pats him on the shoulder. "You do that."

As Eagle hustles over to the bottles of water at the bar, Cole drifts to the corner, out of earshot from the others, and calls Shauna. When she answers, he asks, "Any idea what Gemento wants Rose Stallos and Grant Hampton to admit about the pipeline?"

"I just got off the phone with him. He refused to say. But if Stallos and Hampton don't confess on video within an hour, he's going to shoot another hostage. If they still hold out, he's going to kill another every hour after."

Cole lets out a long exhale. "I don't know much about Rose Stallos, but I've seen enough Grant Hampton speeches to know he's a full-on political operator. If he was involved in some corrupt deal to get the pipeline built, and admitted it, his shot at ever being President would be crushed. I've been deployed on missions thought up by guys like him. The deaths of a few innocent people mean nothing to them compared to their career ambitions. Hampton won't confess."

"I agree," she says, in a disheartened tone.

Cole didn't want the evening to go here, but he seems to have no other options. "In the army, I used a piece of technology that might be able to help."

"What? How?" Her voice has livened up.

"You probably never heard of it. I doubt the federal government has made it available to local law enforcement. I need you to ask your FBI pals for another favor. I need a download link for a certain app, with an authorization code."

"If the FBI knows how to use this thing, why don't we just let them? They have a team of tech experts on call. Why do you need to download it yourself?"

"The app only works if you're on the same Wi-Fi network as the target. It's close range. I'll need to get up close to Gemento."

"Jesus. How are you going to do that without one of the nine remaining terrorists up there putting a bullet in your head?"

21

A round-faced, mid-thirties man cries in the ballroom. He sits on the floor, against the wall, with his thighs pressed to his chest, hugging his shins. His mouth contorts into various shapes as he sobs, a rectangle, an oval, a line. Gemento concludes he's the husband of the dead woman, Melinda. A minute ago, the weeping man received a call and said into the phone, "Yeah, it was Mom."

One of the Stallos employees placed a tablecloth over Melinda's corpse, however, Gemento removed it. He wants Rose and Hampton to see the result of their stalling, the hole in the bridge of the woman's nose, the bits of bone mixed with the blood on her cheeks, her lifeless, still-open eyes.

Off in a corner, Rose and Hampton talk, far enough from other hostages to hear. The conversation seems contentious. Rose, in her designer high heels, stomps the floor. Hampton, with a smug grin, shakes his head.

"I just had a look at the drone," says Hectus, the Iraq vet. His pronounced Adam's apple bulges under his mask as he talks. "We got damn lucky the governor happened to look up. That was a military model with high-end imaging capabilities. The cops were about to—"

"I've got a man watching the sky with binoculars. If they happen to fly anything else over here, he's going to blast it to pieces."

"The cops likely won't come at us with a drone again. They'd go with something new, try to take us by surprise."

"I'd like to see them try, from a mile away."

Hectus crosses his bulky arms. "This plan we came up with, it's been going well so far. But no plans are infallible. After enough time, you can reveal a point of exposure. We—"

"What are you trying to say?"

"We have no idea what the cops could pull next. We also have no idea what's going on in the south wing, right under our goddamn noses. Those are high-risk variables. We've made all the money we need. We have a great exit procedure in place. Why don't—"

"Quit? Is that what you're saying?"

"I wouldn't phrase it that way. We'd be extracting ourselves from a mission at an advantageous point, even if—"

"This mission has two parts. The money is just one. Failing to accomplish both is failure overall."

Hectus lets out an exhale from his nostrils, strong enough to be audible from under the mask. "We can be waiting around all night for the scumbag governor and that slut CEO to confess. All we'd be getting from it is more dead hostages, but the cops would be getting more time. The more they have, the better an offensive they can put together. You want to spend the rest of your life with me and your other brothers in Moldova? Or you want to spend it alone in a federal prison?"

"I didn't start the Children of the Sun to be a burglar. I started it to be a revolutionary. I thought you were one, too."

"I am. But—"

"The only way we're going to start any sort of a movement in America is if those two tell the camera what they did. For the citizens out there to see how rigged this system really is, to see it the way I have, we need to bring the details of an incident like this to light. Then, hopefully, good people will stop standing for this crap."

Hectus looks down for a moment, then back up at Gemento. "What happened with the pipeline was horrible, but with all due respect, what they did only affected you on a personal level, not the rest of us. As much as I want to see Hampton and Rose get what they deserve, I can view this situation with a bit more objectivity than—"

Gemento slams his fist on a dining table, plates and cups rattling. "No."

Nearby hostages glimpse him. An overturned glass of red wine spills, and a stain swells on the white tablecloth.

"Turn the fuck around," he screams. They do. He takes a deep breath, calms his voice, and says to Hectus, "If you want to abandon this mission, if you want to abandon me and your brothers, you can leave now. But then you're done. Don't even consider showing up in Moldova. You won't be welcome. I have the power to let people into this organization. And I have the power to kick them out."

"Okay. I understand. Let's see what the governor and Rose decide to do when their hour is up." He walks away.

The inside of Gemento's ski mask is soaked in sweat, and his pulse bangs in his neck. He has an urge to attack the governor and Rose now, to gouge out their eyes with his thumbs, then dig his fingers through their skulls and tear at their brains until they're dead. But he holds himself back, at least for now.

After getting them to confess, his splendid reward will be murdering them.

22

Shauna goes for a sip from her thermos, but only a drop of coffee is left, just enough to wet her tongue and let her know what she's missing. She thinks about that one thing Gemento said on the livestream, about America's upper class relying on armed police to keep the power structure in place. Gemento seemed to render all cops as mindless enforcers who do whatever politicians demand. He's naive. The job has a lot more to it than that. However, Shauna has been struggling with her responsibilities tonight.

A crisis negotiator, she is paid to prevent hostages from dying, a task she is already failing at. Though she lacked any negotiating leverage leading up to Melinda Raymon's murder, her supervisors don't want excuses. They want results.

She checks the time on her phone. Just thirty-five more minutes until another hostage is up for execution. And no text messages from ballroom captives have come in that suggest Grant Hampton or Rose Stallos is preparing a confession.

Hampton's assistant, a young, pretty brunette, smokes a cigarette under the tent. Earlier, Shauna and other cops were asking her if she knew anything about her boss's involvement in any shady, backroom pipeline deal. The assistant just shook her head, blowing out smoke.

Though the young woman has a government job, just like the cops, she gives off the impression she thinks she's above them. Shauna heard she's from a wealthy family in Helena and went to some fancy school on the East Coast.

The young woman's concern for the hostages seems close to zero. From the few things she's said, her only priority seems to be her boss getting out of there alive, with his reputation intact. Shauna wonders if she even cares about Hampton, or just wants him to stay in power so she can lean on his connections for her own budding political career.

"I just received word from my tech," a female FBI agent says. She wears rectangular glasses, a few snowflakes stuck to the lenses. "The assistant manager has us configured."

"Great," Shauna replies. The feds sent Cole the app he requested. For it to work, a piece of related tracking software needed to be installed on the Alpine Grand's Wi-Fi network, which an off-shift assistant manager, with admin access, was just able to do from his home. "I'll contact our guy on the inside and let him know."

"This man on the inside...Maddox...you've met him before?"

"No."

"What he's about to do...if he happens to succeed, he's going to be in quite an interesting financial position. Are you certain we can trust him in a position like that?"

"No, I'm not certain. But it is my job to negotiate with people on calls. I've talked to all sorts of them over the last decade. I'd like to think I have a pretty good sense of how to judge someone over the phone. And this guy, something about him is just...I don't know...honest."

The fed does not indicate approval or disapproval of this answer. She turns around and walks toward her associate.

Just before Shauna calls Cole, he calls her.

"The app should be fully functional," she says.

"I just saw. Thank you. Time to focus on the next phase."

The app can pick up signals from any phones on the Alpine Grand Wi-Fi network and show them to Cole on a map, each represented with a little red dot. But no identifying information about the devices comes through right away, like their phone numbers. If Cole stands just outside the ballroom, he's going to see over a hundred identical dots. One of them would be Gemento's, but he wouldn't know which.

Cole could enter the ballroom and try to stand next to Gemento, putting his signal nearest, but an outsider waltzing in would provoke suspicion. The terrorists in there would assume he's from the south wing, where they've been running into problems. Within an instant, they may shoot him.

A hard wind shakes the police tent's polyester top. "The next phase is what scares me," Shauna says. "I still don't know how you can realistically sneak into the ballroom and get that close to him without any of them noticing."

"Neither do I. Which is why I say we get him out of the ballroom."

She lifts her thermos, forgetting, for a moment, that it's empty. "To where?"

"There's a restaurant in the north wing, near the main entrance. I can hide in there. All you need to do is get him to walk out of the ballroom into the lobby. That should be enough of a distance for me to isolate his phone signal."

"It is getting late, and he maybe hasn't hit his steps for the day. I'll just call him and tell him I think he's due for a heart-friendly stroll."

"Funny."

Sarcasm is a defense mechanism she developed in high

school. It still sometimes slips out when she's nervous. "Sorry. Okay. Let me think. Gemento, lobby. Gemento...lobby."

"The off-duty assistant manager you spoke to before. He must know the lobby in detail. Maybe he'll have an idea."

That guy was jittery when Shauna called him, traumatized by his trapped coworkers and the livestreamed murder. Though he did upload the tracking software, all he had to do was click a few keys, following steps the FBI provided. What Cole's asking for now requires a more complex form of thinking, one a distressed guy may not be capable of.

No excuses. If Shauna can steer the conversation and ask the right questions, she can get a result. But with the hostage-execution deadline getting close, she needs to hurry.

23

Cole skulks through a hotel corridor with a bulletproof vest, pistol, binoculars, and silenced walkie-talkie taken off the terrorists in the game room. He passes an entryway to an employees-only area. The supply closet, and Diaz, must be back there. Cole heads to a four-way intersection, where the four wings of the cross-shaped resort meet. He continues straight, by a sign for the *North Wing*, to a hallway lined with framed contemporary paintings.

Concealed behind a wall, he listens for voices by the ballroom. Any noise seems muffled behind big, closed doors, nobody in the hall. Unseen, he dashes into the lobby and the restaurant off it, the Four Foxes Cafe.

Closed for the Stallos private event, the lights are off, yet some light from the lobby spills inside, diffused on the four colorful foxes painted on each of the four walls, yellow, purple, green, and pink. He hides behind the bar. At this angle, a mirror on a wall provides a view into the lobby.

He liked how Shauna worked with that assistant manager to come up with a strategy in such a tight time frame. He's known plenty of cops. She's a good one. He takes a deep breath and texts her:

Make the call.

He waits, staring at the mirror. Just fourteen more minutes left until another hostage is shot in the face.

Soon, he hears footsteps. Gemento, with his phone to his ear, appears in the mirror. He kneels in front of the lobby sculpture, the frontiersman with distorted features. He reads the placard at the base. The plan is going as intended.

Then a problem arises.

Another terrorist, trailing Gemento by just a few feet, shows up in the mirror. Gemento could've assumed this was some sort of ambush, so brought some muscle to watch his back.

Cole glimpses the map on the app the FBI gave him. It picks up two nearby phones, however, the red dots representing them are on top of each other. He needs to isolate Gemento's, yet he can't tell which is which. For the app to space out the signals on the map, the two phones need to be at least thirty feet apart.

"Bizno," Gemento says into his phone. "What the hell is that supposed to mean?"

Bizno is the name of the artist who made the sculpture. According to the hotel assistant manager, Bizno is a self-professed socialist who seems to share similar views as the Children of the Sun. The son of an investment banker from Manhattan, the twenty-nine-year-old, tattooed artist resides in the priciest neighborhood in Brooklyn. This sculpture of his, called *West Ward*, is worth a quarter of a million dollars.

Gemento is quiet, as if hearing Shauna out. Per the plan, she is to tell him how valuable the sculpture is and provide the name of a reputable art website where he can verify the information. She is to then tell him he is welcome to take the sculpture and sell it on the black market. In exchange for tipping him off about the art, she is to ask that he refrain from shooting more hostages.

"I don't need any more money," Gemento screams into the

phone. "I have been very clear about what I need. A confession. And I'm not a socialist. That's an even worse system than the one we have. I believe in capitalism, just a version that's fair. No deal, you dumb fucking cop."

He ends the call. He balls his fists and presses them against his hips. He's still for a couple seconds, then kicks over the ceramic sculpture. It cracks on the floor with a high-pitched ding. A diagonal fissure runs across the frontiersman's face. Gemento stomps it into pieces.

Cole and Shauna didn't expect him to go for the deal. They just needed the offer to seem credible enough that the cops would urge him out into the lobby to consider it. Shauna completed her end of the plan. But Cole still lacks an opening to complete his.

The two terrorists turn around and take a few steps toward the ballroom. Cole looks around, noticing an ice machine behind the bar. He chucks a cube across the restaurant. It lands on a table with a clink.

Gemento and his associate stop and unholster their guns. They take slow steps inside the restaurant, veering toward the noise. Once their backs are to Cole, he rises above the bar and flings another ice cube out into the lobby. It bangs off a fragment of the frontiersman's head, another clink.

Cole ducks back down. The terrorists whip their heads toward the noise in the lobby. Gemento taps himself on the chest and points out there, as if to suggest he'll check it out. While he goes that way, the other terrorist continues to search the restaurant, looking under tables as if for anything suspicious.

Cole checks the app's map. The red dots are still on top of each other. He runs a hand through his hair. He needs to get the two phones even farther from each other. The original plan was risky. The modification he's about to add makes it way riskier.

He slides off his hard-soled dress shoes. Though they were useful earlier for knocking an icicle loose, they'd be a burden for what he's about to do, too much noise. He darts out from behind the bar, remaining crouched. In just socks, his feet are quiet. He presses the binoculars to his chest, avoiding them flapping and clunking. Moving from table to table, he approaches the terrorist in the restaurant, staying out of the peripheral vision of him and Gemento.

Cole, who appreciated these men's decision to spare Diaz's life, has killed no terrorists tonight. However, after the execution of Melinda Raymon, his personal rules of engagement have changed.

He lunges toward the back of the terrorist. At this close distance, the man picks up the soft noise of Cole's feet and turns around, preparing to aim his gun. However, before he can complete his 180, Cole grabs the guy's head and snaps his neck.

The man's lifeless fingers let go of his gun. Cole rushes to a knee and catches it right before it strikes the floor with a loud noise. With his other hand, Cole eases the corpse down, then sticks the second Sig Sauer in his tux pants beside the first.

"I don't see anything out here," Gemento says from the lobby. "You?"

Cole pulls the dead terrorist's phone out of his pocket. In the mirror, Gemento turns to come back inside the restaurant. Just before he's seen, Cole sneaks through a set of swinging doors into the kitchen.

Pots and pans hang over commercial-sized ovens and stoves. The scents of strong spices hang in the air. Cole opens a back door and hurls the terrorist's phone out into the snow. When he checks his own phone, he sees a split of the two red dots. He taps on the one for Gemento, then clicks a button labeled *Access*.

What the app is doing requires quite a bit of processing power, and service up on a mountain isn't ideal. A loading bar shows up on Cole's screen, only seven percent done. Any moment, Gemento is going to see his friend's corpse and panic. He may call over some others and check the kitchen for whoever was responsible.

Cole leans outside through the back door. Without his tux jacket, which is still a tourniquet for Diaz, or his shoes, the chill is even harsher than it was before.

Bombs can be anywhere. He must avoid stepping on the ground at all. He climbs on top of the door, then scales the roof. Once perched on the ridge, he checks the app's loading bar. Thirty-two percent. Once loading is complete, the app will produce a mirror of Gemento's phone, which Cole will be able to see without a passcode. Any app or piece of data Gemento has will be accessible to Cole.

However, the time is nearing for another hostage execution.

24

Gemento stares down at the dead member of the Children of the Sun. He removes the man's sunglasses and looks into his stilled green eyes. Gemento recalls the first time they talked, online. The man left a comment on a blog post Gemento wrote, telling him that his insight gave him back the sense of self-worth he lost over twenty years ago, after being battered by a thankless career and a thankless love life. In the past, Gemento would say a prayer at a moment like this, standing over the lifeless body of a friend. But he no longer believes in God.

Hectus scours the Four Foxes Cafe for clues. He's checked under every table, nothing so far. "Huh," he says, standing behind the bar. He crouches and rises with a pair of men's dress shoes.

This piece of garbage must still be close. Gemento bursts through the double doors into the kitchen, his pistol raised, ready to fire at anything human. He looks behind the stainless-steel food-prep table, then inside the walk-in refrigerator. He opens the back door and peers outside. Nobody in sight.

"I'll find him," Hectus says. "But first, it's just about that time."

Gemento grabs the shoes from Hectus and they march to the

ballroom. When they come through the oak doors, hostages cower. None makes eye contact, some hiding underneath tables. The hour is almost up. One of them may die. But first Gemento wants answers.

He stomps toward Rose and Hampton, who back into the wall. Gemento holds up the shoes and shouts, "Whose are they?"

"What?" the governor says.

"Is this who's been causing problems in the south wing?"

"I really have no idea what you're talking about." Hampton turns to Rose. She throws up her hands and shakes her head.

Gemento launches the shoes at them. They duck. The hard soles thud against the wall.

"Whoever he is, whatever he's up to, I assure you it won't work," Gemento says. "He will be found and punished in a hideous fashion." He points at Hectus, who taps a few buttons on his phone and begins recording another livestream. Gemento takes a couple deep breaths, trying to calm himself for the camera. "Welcome back friends. Let's see if Mrs. Stallos and Mister Hampton have wised up." He turns to them. "Would you like to be honest with the American people about what you've done?"

Hampton's fake expression is masterful. He looks into the camera, appearing under control, yet just confused enough to raise doubts about Gemento's accusations against him. Rose, though, no longer seems capable of putting up a facade. The muscles in her face twitch, pulling against her plastic-surgery-tightened skin.

She says nothing. Neither does the governor.

Gemento sets his gaze on his target, a slim man in his thirties with dark hair and blue eyes. Gemento walked past this guy earlier and noticed how manicured his fingernails were. He's in an expensive tuxedo, but somehow doesn't look like he's worked a day in his life. Like the woman he shot before,

Gemento selects a victim from the younger end of the group. Killing someone with a lot of life to live has a more devastating effect.

The slim man sprints toward the oak doors. One of Gemento's guys smashes the butt of a rifle into his sternum. Wheezing, the man collapses. Gemento hooks him under the arms and drags his flailing body to the center of the room. His date, a young brunette in red, wails.

When Gemento sticks the barrel of his gun against the man's temple, Rose blurts, "No."

Hampton gives her a stern look, as if trying to warn her against whatever she's about to say. Though the predominant emotion in her employees' faces remains fear, a hint of curiosity crops up in some.

"You're ready to talk?" Gemento asks.

She doesn't say yes, but her eyes hint that she's about to. Hampton, with an even sterner expression, whispers something in her ear.

The man with the primped fingernails thrashes in Gemento's headlock. Gemento feels something else against his body, something subtler. His phone is vibrating. He holsters his gun and checks the screen. That woman-cop negotiator, who must be watching the livestream.

Now that she saw Rose might confess, she could want to discuss a hostage-release plan. Gemento passes the headlocked guy to one of his men and answers the call.

"The CEO isn't enough," Gemento says. "Even if she does admit what she did, no hostage is leaving here unless the governor does, too."

"I've got a better idea," the female cop says. "How about you let all the hostages go? In return, we'll give you back some of your money."

"Excuse me?"

"Not the entire two point seven million. But I can get authorization for a million. I strongly advise you take this offer."

"You're giving me money I...what?"

"Check the CryptoLX app on your phone and call me when you come to your senses." She hangs up.

Hectus, staring at him, must infer something is off, because he stops recording the livestream. "Who was that?"

Gemento is silent, his heart banging. With a tentative hand, he taps the CryptoLX icon on his phone. His balance is zero. One minute ago, all of the Bitcoin was transferred to an account called *Gotcha*.

25

Hampton paces away from the other hostages, waves over Rose and Ollie, and says to her in a loud whisper, "If you cave to these White trash cretins, it's going to be career suicide. You were about a second away, I saw it in your face. Fuck, Rose."

She holds her throat, stroking the side with her thumb. Ollie stares at her. She looks radiant even when stressed. He has been in love with her since he met her. Back then, she was married, so he hesitated to tell her. However, once her husband died, the thought of ending up with her became somewhat realistic, even though Rose is out of his league from both a physical and wealth standpoint. He's grown more and more distant from his wife ever since.

But Ollie's been too afraid to admit his love for Rose. Her rejecting him would be a blow of finality. For the last couple of years, each of his days has been a little better because the hope of ending up with Rose was real. Avoiding telling her his feelings has kept him from dating her, yet also kept the hope alive.

The terrorists, reacting to that phone call Gemento just received, haven't gone through with their second murder. The young executive who had the gun to his head is slumped in a chair, still panting, his wife dabbing his face with a wet napkin. Gemento is off in the corner with the brawny terrorist in the form-fitted shirt, who seems to be his second in command, and a couple others. Though Ollie can't hear them from here, their body language suggests they're arguing.

Ollie glances at the pair of shoes thrown into the wall. He has a feeling who they belong to. He texts Cole:

Are you the one pissing them off?

Cole replies:

We have their crypto. This will hopefully all be over soon.

Ollie smiles. Son of a bitch. He knew that guy was different ever since he saved his coworker from that pipe.

Rose takes antsy steps in a tight circle, texting on a chain with her two grown children. They didn't go into the family business, neither here tonight. Supported with considerable trust funds, the son is a ski instructor in Vail and the daughter an aspiring musician in Los Angeles. Hampton appears to be meditating, his eyes closed, his middle fingers touching his thumbs.

"At this point, don't confess anything," Ollie says to them. He informs them that the ex-commando on the property, who seems to be working with the cops, somehow stole the terrorists' money as leverage.

"A fucking commando is here to rescue me," Hampton says, with a haughty grin. "Can you believe that? I knew I'd come out of this okay. I've been manifesting a positive outcome, like I always do, and here it is. Mental positivity, that's the key to success."

Rose doesn't appear excited like him, but pensive. "How is a deal with the crypto supposed to work?"

"My guess is the terrorists get a chance to leave the hotel, if they go ASAP," Ollie says. "Once they're off the grid, they tell the cops the location of the explosives. When the hostages are cleared out, the terrorists get back a portion of the money."

"And, what, just get away with this?" She points at Melinda's bloody body. "No prison time? No...justice?"

"Rose, sweetheart," Hampton says. "It's negotiating. Give and take, baby." He snaps his fingers a couple times. "Do you want these guys to stick around until you end up like that poor broad on the rug with half her face missing? My good man Oliver is saying the terrorists will leave soon, if this deal goes down. Meaning, nobody will be here to force us to admit anything on camera. Who cares about some vague principle like justice? That's something losers go around complaining about. Not someone like you, Rose. It's unbecoming. Really."

He is at least right about Rose not being a loser. She is a terrific CEO. Still, Stallos Energy's other C-level executives wanted her out since the day she was named boss. They convinced the board of directors to give her outrageous targets for the company's stock price. If she were treated like a normal CEO, with normal goals, she wouldn't have had to cheat to boost the stock's value.

What she, Hampton, and Ollie did to get the pipeline approved was wrong. But the contract put Hampton in the Governor's Mansion for a second term and Rose in the good graces of her board.

"I understand what negotiating is," she says to Hampton. "I'm in charge of a multi-billion-dollar corporation." She watches Gemento in the corner, quarreling with his crew. "But it doesn't look like this negotiation is going well. I don't think they're going to accept any deal. Then what?"

26

Cole hides behind a hotel suite's chimney on the roof of the east wing. Climbing balconies, he reached the third story. From this elevated view, he's noticed the storm has toppled a couple small trees around the property and snapped branches off larger ones.

His shoeless feet sting from the cold wind. His elbows hooked over the roof ridge, he peers with his binoculars through a north-wing window, at the hallway just outside the ballroom. As of now, the hall is empty. But he suspects that may change soon.

In the solitude up here, his mind drifts to Lacey. Studying all night, she must've not caught the local news before bed. If she did, she would've contacted him, panicking about the terrorists. By the time she wakes up in the morning, he hopes to have all this resolved. He wishes he were with her in their warm bed. She's switched to sleeping on her left side, which the OB-GYN doctor recommended for pregnancy. He lies on his right, facing her, and falls asleep with his hand on her stomach.

He texts Shauna:
Anything yet from them on your offer?
She replies:

Nothing.

He was almost certain the Children of the Sun would've accepted her deal by now. But enough time has passed to sour that optimism. If the missing crypto isn't enough to convince them to give up the hostages, he should try to gain more leverage.

He opens the FBI's mirroring program and eyes the apps on Gemento's home screen. CryptoLX seems to be the only non-default one. The text messages are just as stripped down as those of the terrorists tied up in the game room. However, something is in the photos area.

Three pictures. All of the same woman, a pretty blonde. In the first, she's in her mid-twenties. In a striped, one-piece bathing suit on a white-sand beach, she nudges her sunglasses down on her button nose, revealing the top halves of her blue eyes. She pouts her lips, like a model pose, however, does with an air of irony, the edge of her mouth breaking into a smirk.

In the second photo, she appears about ten years older. She's in the den of a quaint home. It looks a bit like Cole's living room. A toy tractor is on the floor. She's in shorts and slippers, her feet up on the coffee table, a huge fleece blanket on her top half, one arm poking out with a big cup of coffee. Her hair, in a ponytail, is a bit messy. She looks up at the camera in surprise, her mouth opening as if to call off the candid photo.

She's about forty in the last picture. Though still beautiful, she has some age lines around her eyes. She's in the same den of the quaint home, an Airedale terrier at her side, a fireplace aglow. In a green sweater, she hangs an ornament on a Christmas tree, smiling for the camera over her shoulder.

The pictures have nothing to do with Gemento's siege of the hotel. He must've put them on his phone for some personal reason. Whatever the case, if the authorities' facial-recognition software could ID this woman, they may be able to use the intel to

ID Gemento. Cole sends the three photos to Shauna, with the context.

He looks down at the icon on his own phone for CryptoLX. The balance of his Gotcha account is $2,725,000 of Bitcoin. With the tap of just a few buttons, he could convert the Bitcoin into US dollars, then transfer them to his personal bank account. He could become a multimillionaire in minutes.

Lacey's boy, Declan, does have some cash in his name from his late biological father. However, none of that is hers, Cole's, or their daughter's. Embezzling the funds would help them all.

With his Special Forces skill set, Cole could pull something like this off. The moment he found out where the bombs were, he'd escape the property. The authorities would, of course, know he ran off with the money and come after him. But he could evade them. With a bit more deception, he'd flee America with Lacey and her son to a non-extradition country and begin a new life there.

Overseas, a dollar can go even further than here. His daughter could have the best of everything. They could live like the family of a wealthy Stallos executive.

27

Gemento, Hectus, and two other Children of the Sun speak in the ballroom corner with the pile of jazz instruments. Hectus is pissed at Gemento for not leaving with the money while they had it. However, the other two don't blame Gemento for this mess. They agreed with the decision to stick around to force a confession out of Rose and Hampton. The slut and the scumbag.

"Your phone," Hectus says to Gemento. "They must've somehow gotten into it." As mad as Hectus is, he keeps his composure. If they're going to get through this, they need to continue working as a team.

"How is that even possible?"

"Years ago, when I was in the service, the government had some pretty spooky tracking technology. I can only imagine what they've got today. If you want to get out of a hole, the first thing to do is stop digging. Shut it off and break it."

Gemento gazes down at his phone. On it are three photos he's been glancing at through the night. They're a reminder of why getting justice on Rose and Hampton is so important. Hectus, though, is right. The phone must go. Gemento turns it off and bashes it with the leg of a chair.

"Now that our vulnerability is gone," one of his men says, in his early thirties, "let's just jack these Stallos people for another twenty-five K each. They're loaded. They'll give it."

"If one of our phones was compromised, another could be," Hectus says. "We'd run the risk of getting robbed again. We need a more definitive solution."

"They may have the crypto, but we still have the hostages," Gemento says. "We're still in a stronger negotiating position than them. We're still on top."

"But if we kill another hostage, the cops' deal for a mil goes off the table," the early-thirties one says. "We should—"

"That million has got to be a bluff," Hectus says. "Once we give them the location of the bombs, they ain't giving us shit. We're going for the full two point seven two five million, right here."

"You expect the cops to just give us all the money back, without—"

"The cops aren't even part of the conversation as far as I'm concerned. They don't have the money." Hectus points at the pair of shoes he found in the restaurant. "He does. He could be running some close-range hacking program on his phone."

"Even if he got into my phone," Gemento says, "he wouldn't know where the explosives are planted. He's still trapped on the property."

"It's simple," Hectus says. "We find him. We capture him. We torture him until he transfers the money from his account back into ours."

"If we get the crypto that way, we won't need to let any hostages go," Gemento says. "We still can still squeeze the slut and the scumbag into an on-camera confession."

"Sounds great," the early-thirties guy says. "But we need to find the prick first. How we supposed to do that?"

"He's obviously not wearing any shoes," Hectus says. "You

see a guy anywhere out there in socks, open fire. Legs, arms. Nothing fatal. We can bloody him up, but still need him alive. At least until he hands over what he took. Then I'll kill him myself."

"Who the fuck do you think this guy is?"

Hectus goes quiet for a few seconds and nods at the Stallos crowd. "I no longer think he's one of them. He seems to have some type of operational background."

The man hangs his head, as if worrying.

"But that won't be a problem," Hectus says. "I've trained you all, too. And there's one of him and a lot of us."

The man nods, then eyeballs the hostages. "Is it just me, or do these entitled sacks of shit seem a little more relaxed, after we came over here to talk instead of dropping a second body?"

"We can't let them think this asshole made us go soft," Gemento says.

Hectus walks up to the closest guy in a tuxedo under forty and blasts a bullet through the back of his head.

28

Cole, still perched on the east wing's roof, didn't transfer any of the Bitcoin into his bank account. Though the sum would change his family's lives, and the $25,000 chunks would not change the lives of the Stallos employees, they still deserve their money back after this is all over. They worked for it, not Cole. If he embezzled it, he'd be a criminal, not much better than the terrorists. Plus, he doesn't want to raise his family overseas. The USA is his home. Yes, the country has its problems, but he loves it and still believes it's the best on earth.

Shauna calls him. "What's up?" he says.

"Good news and bad."

"You pick the order."

"We just got a report from inside. Another hostage. Curtis Fitts. Point-blank, back of the skull."

Cole takes a long breath of freezing air. "Safe to say that's a no-go on your deal."

"If they're not going for my deal, they're going to come looking for—"

"I know."

"You going to be all right over there all by yourself?"

"We'll see."

"Well, now for the good news. We got a face scan back on that woman from Gemento's phone. Her name was Ella Laud."

"Was?"

"Car accident, eleven months ago. Her fault. Her blood alcohol level was four times the legal limit. Drove her Chevy off a mountain road, slid down a hill, and slammed into a boulder. Died on impact."

Cole thinks back to her photos. Those vibrant blue eyes, they reminded him a bit of Lacey's. This woman, Ella Laud, didn't seem like some reckless drunk.

"So who was she?" he asks.

"She graduated high school twenty-seven years ago just outside Missoula. She sold hand-painted stuff on Etsy. Coffee mugs, keychains, that sort of thing. Nineteen years ago, she married a man named William Laud."

"You think that's Gemento?"

"Obviously, with the mask, we can't do a facial match. But we did find a driver's license in the database for him, with his height on it. Six three."

That's what Gemento is. William Laud. Gemento is William Laud.

"What else did you find on him?" Cole asks.

"He used to own Laud Farm, a fifth-generation family business in Gallatin County. A bunch of fairly recent DEQ records came up in the system. Department of Environmental Quality. The year before last, they found excessive amounts of fertilizer in the farm's water. William Laud racked up a hefty fine each day the problem wasn't resolved. He couldn't seem to get it under control. He sold the farm. I'm guessing he needed the proceeds to pay off the fines."

"Huh. Who'd he sell it to?"

"Not much on them. Some investment holding company.

Horizon Land Corp. We emailed the lawyer listed on the paperwork. Left a voicemail, too, but haven't heard back yet."

"Any criminal history on William Laud?"

"Just a couple speeding tickets over the years. Nothing at all to indicate he's capable of terrorism. What could help, though, he has a son. William Junior. Seventeen."

"The police are with him?"

"Unfortunately, not yet. Can't get him on the phone. After he and his father moved off the farm, we don't have a current address. We're trying to figure out what school the kid goes to, see if we can get a location through them. If so, I want to patch him onto a call with his father. These situations are often just as high-stress for the perps as they are the hostages. Hearing the voice of a family member can go a long way. I'm hoping the kid can talk down his dad."

"Agreed." Cole recalls those three photos of Ella Laud. Gemento must've taken them. That toy tractor on the floor must've belonged to William Junior. "In the pictures, they seemed like a nice family. Difficult to imagine how it all somehow turned to...this."

"I was thinking the same thing. Gemento...William Laud, whatever you want to call him...must've really loved Ella, if he went out of his way to put those photos of her on his burner tonight. Among all this craziness, a part of him still needed to remind himself of those memories. But with her gone, seeing the pictures has got to be hard, too. Like looking at a distance into some sort of frozen dream."

Cole is silent for a moment. "Keep me posted on any developments."

"Same."

After the call ends, he enters "Laud Farm" into a search engine. On a map, he sees where in Gallatin County it's situated.

He's familiar with the area. He's seen it on documents at work. The Stallos Energy pipeline is planned to run right through it.

Cole isn't certain how yet, but various pieces must come together in some way to form a holistic picture. Contaminated water, state-issued fines, the governor, the sale of Laud Farm to some anonymous investment company, the Stallos pipeline, the Stallos CEO, a dead wife, a vengeful husband.

Though Cole opposes the terroristic response, he does sense William Laud, AKA Gemento, was exploited in some way. If a small farmer butted up against the state government and a multi-billion-dollar energy corporation, in all likelihood, the small farmer would end up crushed.

Through the binoculars, Cole picks up activity inside the hotel. Four terrorists, two clutching rifles, march out of the ballroom. They must be searching for him.

Cole does have two pistols at his waist, but at this distance, with the storm's high wind, pistol shots wouldn't be accurate. If he fired one, the sound would give away his position and the rifle shots returned could be accurate.

Numbers and limited weapon use aren't his only disadvantages in this fight. He lacks a jacket and shoes in near-zero weather. Not to mention, to avoid getting blown up, he must avoid the entire ground.

If he is going to edge out these terrorists hunting for him, he must be just as crafty as he is deadly.

29

Cole, through windows, watches the four terrorists look for him in the north wing. They go in and out of the bellhop area, conference rooms, and bathrooms. If Cole returned to the north wing for an offensive, he'd tangle himself in a four-on-one fight. Even if he were more skilled than them, an imbalance of opponents in close quarters would be difficult to overcome. His odds in a pair of two-on-one confrontations would be better than those in a single four-on-one. He needs to split them up.

He slides down the slanted roof and lands on the balcony of the third-story suite he's been above. The piled-up snow engulfs his feet. He yanks on the glass door. Locked. He whacks the pane with the handle of a gun, splintering it, then elbows loose enough shards to reach inside and unlock the door.

The suite's warmth provides a shred of comfort to his soaked, freezing body. He dries himself off with a towel. Light from a night-table lamp carries into the dark bathroom, bringing out his reflection in the mirror. His dirty-blond hair is strewn about, some strands icy. His jaw is bruised, dry blood around his mouth.

He checks the room for shoes and clothing, but its only guest appears to be female, just a few of her items in the closet. He jogs through the hallway to a stairwell, which he takes to the first floor, then continues toward the intersection of the hotel's four wings.

From the wall, he rips a framed contemporary painting and bashes it against the floor, just before the east wing meets the intersection. A jumble of glass slivers shoots all over the rug. He picks one up, rolls up a pantleg, and slices his calf. Just deep enough for blood to trickle. He lets some pool on his fingers, then smears it on a few pieces of broken glass by the painting, which is blank other than some text in the center in comic-book font, *YOU'RE SMART & BEAUTIFUL.*

He dashes through the intersection on to the west wing and passes a leather bench, the frosted-glass entrance to the hotel's spa, and some guest rooms. Into the walkie-talkie, he says, "Anyone there? It's the guy you're looking for."

The yellow-and-black radio is silent for half a minute. Then a male voice asks, "Where are you?"

"I'm about to tell you. But first, I want to make sure we're on the same page."

Again, the walkie-talkie is quiet for a while, as if the man on the other end is conferring with his associates before answering. "Send back the money, every last penny. If you're not willing to do that, we're not willing to have a conversation."

"That's exactly what I'm willing to do. The cops have been demanding a lot of me. They thought you guys would go for the crypto deal. Once you didn't, I was done. I didn't sign up for any of this. I don't care about any of these hostages. I just want to get out of here alive."

"Give us the money and we'll let you live."

"I'm going to need something in return more than your word." He looks around, noting the number of a nearby room. "Meet me in room one eighty-nine. You can watch me transfer the money back into your account. What I want in exchange is a drawn-out map of where the bombs are. I'm not going to show it to anyone else. It's just so I can walk out of here myself. The hostages will stay. Do whatever you want with them. It's now or never. If I don't see you in one eighty-nine in the next five minutes, I'm leaving."

He waits for a reply. The silence lasts long.

30

Vayos, a code name, huddles with three other Children of the Sun in the north wing. Gemento and Hectus, still inside the ballroom, trusted Vayos to be on the team sent after the crypto thief. The tall, fit twenty-nine-year-old excelled during combat training for this mission, earning respect within his organization.

The Children of the Sun saved Vayos's life. He doesn't want to let the others down. Since dropping out of high school at sixteen, Vayos worked in the warehouse of a chemical plant. A few years ago, he developed some odd health issues that crop up from time to time. Blood in his piss. Thunderous headaches. Seizures.

Others at the plant had experienced similar problems, but when they accused their employer of a hazardous work environment, the company brought in a legion of big-city lawyers to delegitimize the claims.

Vayos left and found a job in another warehouse. However, the sporadic seizures turned him into a safety hazard. His new coworkers refused to be around him while transporting material or operating machinery. He was let go. And became unemployable in the only profession he ever knew.

Living alone in a trailer, he soon turned to meth. He was on the verge of withering away from his addiction when he discovered the Children of the Sun on an internet forum. Their messaging made him realize that he was not a failure. Rather, the system was the failure. Once accepted as a member, he moved to Montana and got sober. He's looking forward to the rest of his life in Moldova with his brothers.

"I ain't trust this guy," Vayos says.

"I don't either," the oldest of the foursome says. The thick hair of his arms shows in the small spaces between his sleeves and gloves.

Vayos, who lacked a great memory even before his health issues, struggles to remember all the guys' code names. But he does know the hairy-armed one couldn't find work, just like him. The fortysomething was laid off, losing his pension. He went on something like thirty interviews for new jobs, but got squat. According to him, he wasn't the problem, but an influx of lower-qualified Black and brown applicants who were given jobs because of some special treatment by the government.

"Worst case, we go down to room one eighty-nine and he asks for the bomb map before handing over the money," the fortysomething says. "We won't fall for it. He'll be stuck in a room, four of us, one of him. We pin him down and inflict pain until he gives back the cash, just like the original plan."

"What if he rigged room one eighty-nine with explosives? We open the door, kapow."

"The only explosives on this property are the ones we planted. And this asshole still has no clue where they are. If he did, he wouldn't have hit us up over the radio. He would've hightailed it out of here and not looked back. Chances are, he really does want to make a side deal and save his own ass."

"He's probably some dude who happens to be ex-army," another guy says in his Southern accent. "Somehow, he got invited to this thing. Why would he want to keep risking his life to protect some douchebag oil executives? He wants to get out of here. And to do that, he needs a map from us. We've got the power, not him."

The Southern guy's biological brother is the fourth man in the huddle. They're a pair of Louisiana boys about Vayos's age. Vayos was friends with them even before they all moved to Montana. After meeting online, they'd send each other videos. Some, of course, called out the crooked people who run America, but most of them had nothing to do with business or politics. They were just plain funny. Once, a Louisiana boy sent him a video of this dog who was watching TV and trying to mimic the facial expressions of the actors. It was so good.

The fortysomething waves them all down the hallway toward 189. They move as a unit, their backs facing each other, with three hundred sixty degrees of visibility as a team, their weapons on the ready, just like Hectus taught them in training drills deep in the Montana wilderness.

Soon, they reach the intersection where the four wings meet. According to a sign on the wall, 189 is down the west wing. The eldest hand-signals them that direction.

"What the fuck is that?" mutters the Louisiana boy facing east.

The team stops and looks that way. On the diagonal-striped rug, about ten feet away, is a painting in a broken frame. Vayos kneels beside it for a closer look. Red marks streak some of the glass shards. They seem to be blood.

"You think the blood is from any of the three guys we sent out earlier?" the Louisiana boy asks.

"Maybe," the eldest replies. "Or maybe one of our guys got loose and whacked the thief with the frame. The blood could be his."

"Don't you think our guy would've told us?"

"Not if his walkie-talkie was taken. The thief contacted us on one."

"If they fought, the blood could be from them both. Both could be hurt, holed up somewhere."

The eldest gazes down the east-wing corridor at the doors of guest rooms. "Possibly sending us the opposite direction, to one eighty-nine in the west, could've just been a scheme, a way to get some distance between him and us while he recovered. If so, better to get to him soon, while he's hurt and vulnerable."

"Should we ditch the one-eighty-nine thing and check these rooms instead?" Vayos asks. "We can shoot our way in from outside, you know...like, through the windows."

The eldest grunts. "Or...nobody is badly injured, and this picture frame was just from some minor dust-up before. The thief could be fine, waiting for us in one eighty-nine to give over the money, just like he said. If he's for real and we let the five minutes go by, he'll dip."

"So, what then? We go west?"

The eldest grunts louder than before. "Both." He points at Vayos. "You and me, we'll head west to one eighty-nine." He points at the Louisiana brothers with the rifles. "You two blast your way into the east-wing rooms by the painting. If you find him, incapacitate him, zip-tie him, and get at me on the radio. Got it?"

They nod.

The eldest says into his walkie-talkie, "We're on our way."

31

Two terrorists with pistols trot down the west wing toward room 189. The guy in front is bigger, about Cole's size, while the one in back is average height, but built solid.

Cole hides behind a wall inside the spa, just to the side of the door. It was locked, so he busted through the frosted glass with the handle of his gun, then propped it open, facing in. In a treatment room, he found a circular mirror with a flexible neck, which the staff must use for things like facials. He watches the approaching enemies in it.

A single light is on in the spa, a small one at the base of a clear-glass waterfall in the waiting area. Shadows drape the sofa, reception desk, and shelves on the walls, which are filled with expensive products like vials of exotic oils, metallic astrological symbols, and scented eye masks.

The sound of a rifle shot, outside to the east, disrupts the silence. The two terrorists don't seem fazed by it. Cole's plan to split up the foursome seems to have worked, the others searching for him in eastward rooms. However, he still has a long way to go if he wants to leave this hotel with all his body parts attached.

Cole sets down the mirror and reaches his right hand, wrapped in a towel he took off a massage table, into his pocket for a triangular shard of frosted glass, from the cracked door pane. He holds it with a tight grip, the towel protecting his palm from its sharp edges.

The terrorists' shadows darken the strip of light spilling onto the spa floor. Cole takes a quiet step into the hallway, his feet still in just socks. His enemies, on their way to room 189, their backs facing him, don't see or hear.

Cole spikes the glass triangle into the side of the shorter man's neck. Spurting blood darkens the white towel. The guy drops to his knees and lets out a rasp. Cole would've liked to have penetrated the jugular, but the guy was walking a bit too fast for a sufficient angle. Though he will bleed to death within minutes, he's still alive, still a threat.

Cole kicks the gun out of his hand, banging it into the wall. The taller terrorist spins around, moving his pistol toward Cole. Though rifles going off to the east seem part of the Children of the Sun's strategy, pistols going off to the west would cause alarm, the others rushing over to assist.

Too far from the taller terrorist to grab his gun, Cole snaps loose the towel, holding onto one end, and whips the other into his opponent's barrel, knocking it to the side before he can fire. The man tries to readjust his aim, but before he can, Cole knots the towel around the gun and the hand grasping it.

Over his shoulder, Cole sees the stabbed one stumbling toward his loose pistol. Cole backsteps, yanking the taller enemy with him, keeping his gun hand angled down toward the floor. Right before the stabbed guy picks up his weapon, Cole kicks it into the spa. The marble floor should carry it far, buying him some time.

The taller terrorist punches Cole's wrist with his free hand, trying to break loose from the towel. Cole withstands repeated hits, dragging the guy into the spa. The man throws a left hook, which Cole's occupied hands can't block it, and the fist bashes his forehead.

Cole totters into the shelved wall. A couple bottles of oil fall off and break. The stabbed terrorist looks around for his gun in the shadowy waiting area, crawling with a trail of blood behind him. Though his movements have slowed, he still has the strength to pull a trigger.

The taller opponent slugs Cole in the forehead again, even harder, causing him to let go of the towel. The terrorist lifts his freed gun. However, before he lines up a shot, Cole grabs a six-inch, metal Scorpio symbol off a shelf and slams it into his face. The ends of the two straight parts burst apart the lenses of his sunglasses.

As the man yells in agony, Cole whacks the pistol out of his hand with the Scorpio. The guy's fingers are frantic over his face, as if trying to pull broken bits of his sunglasses out of his eyeballs. Cole notices the other squirming across the floor, just part of him visible from behind the couch. The terrorist has spotted his gun, just a few feet away.

Cole throws the Scorpio into the base of the glass waterfall. It shatters, flooding onto the marble. The terrorist slips. The taller one, groping around as if blinded, staggers out of the spa into the hallway and runs east. Cole debates chasing him, but the stabbed man gets back up on his hands and knees and crawls even closer to his gun. The fight this guy has in him impresses Cole. A shame he chose to fight for such a bad cause.

The man's hand splashes against the floor. Then his other hand. Just before he reaches the gun, Cole snaps his neck. The corpse drops to the marble with an even bigger splash.

Cole strides to the doorway as fast as he can without falling on the wet surface and looks east. The blinded terrorist is out of sight.

32

Cole flips on the radio on his hip. No sound comes from it. Now that his enemies know he has a walkie-talkie, they must've been smart enough to switch the channel they talk on. The long corridor is empty. A series of shadows crosses the rug in the spaces between the wall lamps. But the hall won't stay vacant for long. On the new channel, the blinded one must've gotten a message to the pair to the east that Cole is in the spa.

He needs to hide out in a guest room, but the west wing's first-floor ones will be the first the terrorists check, shooting their way in from outside. Third-floor rooms would be hardest for them to access, but the elevator and stairwell are at the other end of the hall. If Cole went over there, he could run into the hostiles approaching from the east.

He darts through the spa and finds an exterior door that leads to the northwest courtyard. It has a pool, covered for the winter, and three active Jacuzzis, each under a pavilion shielding it from the weather. A few empty beer bottles sit on the edge of a hot tub. The hotel's cleaning staff must've been taken hostage before having a chance to collect them.

Avoiding any bombs on the ground, Cole climbs to the top of

the spa door, hoists himself via the gutter onto the one-story roof, and scrabbles up to its ridge. The warmth he had inside is lost, replaced with a deep chill.

The west wing rises to three stories toward the intersection. If he can traverse the icy, slanted roof there, he can climb balconies to a third-floor suite and break in. He starts moving, his hands and feet buried in the snow, negotiating shingles. Chunks of ice and roof spray into the air inches in front of him. The noise of a rifle shot reverberates from the east.

Cole drops his body and swings it the opposite direction. Clinging to the ridge with one hand, he lifts the binoculars to his face with the other and searches for the threat. Inside, two terrorists aim rifles at him through a shattered window.

Cole ducks his head and lets himself slide down the roof. But before he's out of the line of fire, another round roars this way and rips through his left forearm.

He tries to ignore the searing pain, focusing on not falling to the ground and landing on an explosive. His legs fly off the roof. His uninjured arm swipes at the gutter. He clasps it, his fingers crushing the ice on the edge. Though his left arm aches, it's still somewhat functional, so he grabs the gutter with it, too.

Blood streaks down the sleeve of his white shirt. The two riflemen are sure to be running over here, ready to finish off their wounded target. Based on the length of the corridor, and an athletic running speed, Cole estimates they should arrive in no longer than twenty seconds.

He looks toward the room balconies. No way he can climb to one within twenty seconds with a bullet in him. Instead, he goes the other direction, toward the Jacuzzis. The knuckles of his injured arm quiver. He stops across from the closest hot tub, swings forward, then back, forward, then back and lets go of the gutter. Soaring, he yanks one of the Sig Sauers from his waist and extends it over his head.

His ribcage crashes down onto the edge of the Jacuzzi. A dense pain punches through his torso. His bottom half splashes into the hot, bubbling water. The gun at his waist is soaked, no longer reliable, but he's kept the other dry.

About twelve more seconds until the enemies come out to the courtyard. Cole sets the working pistol on the top step of the Jacuzzi, out of view from the spa doorway. He plunges the whole of himself under the water, clutching the binoculars against his chest so they don't float to the surface and give him away. The chlorine stings the inside of his nose.

He counts in his head. Seven, six, five. Once the countdown is over, he remains submerged a few more seconds, a buffer for any possible delay the terrorists might have had. Then he springs up from the water.

The riflemen are searching the courtyard for him. The closer one notices Cole emerge. As Cole reaches for his gun on the step, the guy turns to him, aiming his rifle. Cole gets off a shot first, blowing a hole through the guy's ski mask.

The second terrorist's rifle is aimed at Cole's chest. Cole dives under the water, keeping his pistol above it. He hears a gunshot. Bits of wood from a blown-apart pavilion post scatter the surface.

Cole adjusts the position of his Sig a few millimeters, aiming at a target he cannot see under the water, going off only a brief visual memory. He squeezes the trigger. His heart galloping, he rises. The second rifleman is splayed on the ground. Like the other, he's still, yet their blood moves, reddening the white of their masks and the snow around their heads.

Three dead and one blind, the foursome of hostiles sent for him have been dealt with. However, this is far from over.

With his wounded forearm, climbing to a guest room from outside carries a falling risk, no longer a good idea. He'll need to find a place to hide from inside. He should have a bit of time before the terrorists in the ballroom deduce their colleagues' failure and send more after him.

Since the riflemen stepped around any bombs, Cole jumps off the edge of the Jacuzzi toward the nearer one and lands in his footprints. Cole picks up the guy's rifle and jogs his path back into the hotel.

33

The dry sensation in Hectus's mouth is reminiscent of his time in the Iraqi basement, where his captors would force him to go full days without fluids. But tonight he's had plenty of water. He supposes he's nervous, a sign of weakness he wouldn't admit to anyone.

He stands with his muscular arms folded, staring out at the Stallos employees in the ballroom. These limp-dicked men in their tailored tuxedos, he'd say the luck of birth got nine out of ten of them the cushy lives they have, not any talent.

If you're born into a family with some bucks, as long as you're not a complete fuckup, the school system winds up getting you into college, and mommy and daddy cover the bill. When you graduate, mommy and daddy's friend from the country club gets you a job in some corporate office. As long as you smile and nod like a bitch every time your boss asks you to do something, you'll wind up getting promoted over time. You don't need to be inventive. You don't need to take risks.

Hectus would like to see how well this crew would've done in the Middle East, plopped in a desert with nothing to rely on but their own instincts. America was settled by men who knew how to perform well in situations like that. Talented, capable men started this country, and ran it for quite a while. Hectus wonders where we all went wrong.

Gemento paces, gazing down at the walkie-talkie in his hand as if trying to will it to issue some good news. They've heard nothing since Vayos reported a surprise attack from the spa. Before joining the Children of the Sun, nobody ever told Vayos he was good at anything. He may not be a genius, but he has grit. Hectus wanted him to succeed. Not just to get the crypto back, but because it would've built up some confidence in the kid.

"Anything, guys?" Hectus asks, into his radio.

The channel is quiet for a while. Then Vayos replies, "They yelled something 'bout shooting him in the arm. I think they ran after him. But that was at least like a few minutes ago and...I ain't heard back since."

"You didn't go with them?"

"Nah, couldn't."

"What do you mean?"

"My eyes. I don't think they work no more."

Hectus's brothers, with their limited tactical experience, have exhibited great fortitude tonight, but a combat veteran like him seems to be needed to regain control of this situation.

"Yo," Hectus says, pointing at a Children of the Sun member. "Come with me."

"Hold on," Gemento says to Hectus. "Three of us went missing in the south wing. One is dead in the restaurant. Another three are now unresponsive. And Vayos is what...fucking blind? We're down to just four active men. I can't risk losing two more, especially if one is you."

"We really can't risk this guy being on the loose any longer. We're more exposed with our lower headcount. If he's as good as he seems to be, he could drop even more bodies. I need to shut his ass down now. And I can't do it from here."

Gemento lets out a long exhale.

"I'll make it back here alive," Hectus says. "You have my word."

Gemento peers up at the chandelier for a while, then nods. Hectus lets his colleague take the only rifle left in here, trusting himself with just a pistol.

"Vayos, where are you?" Hectus asks into his walkie-talkie, exiting the ballroom.

"They put me on a chair. East wing."

Hectus says to his colleague, "We should go different directions. If this guy pulls another ambush, only one of us will be affected."

The man forces down a nervous swallow. "Okay."

"I'll go east. You head south, where this problem started. Maybe someone down there knows who the hell the thief is. If we can ID him, we can put pressure on him from the outside."

The man nods. Hectus points toward the hotel hallways' intersection. Once there, he gives his colleague an encouraging pat on the shoulder and they go their own ways.

A cold wind blows inside. A floor-to-ceiling window is shattered, snow accumulating on the burgundy-and-gold carpet.

Nearby is more broken glass, from a cracked painting frame. Beyond that, on a leather bench, not a chair, is Vayos. His mask is spotted with blood, a few black fragments of his sunglass lenses stuck to the fabric.

As Hectus approaches, Vayos does not seem to notice. His eyeballs are swollen, bulging under his closed lids with a slight tremble.

"Hey buddy," Hectus says.

Vayos smiles. He flails his hand until it meets Hectus's forearm. He squeezes it. "I'm sorry if I let you down with—"

"I don't want to hear that crap. This man took a bullet. He's hurt. If it wasn't for you, that never would've happened."

Vayos nods. He seems proud of this. "Nate, can—"

"No real names."

"Right. My bad." Vayos whacks himself quite hard in the forehead with his palm. "Stupid. I'm so fucking stupid sometimes. I don't know why I'm like that."

"Don't worry about it. Nobody heard. Just, try not to do it again."

"Hey, can I ask you a question?"

"Of course."

"You think the doctors over there, in Moldova, you think they're going to be able to fix my eyes?"

"Sure," Hectus says, though he is far from certain.

"When we're over there, I want to go on walks more. When I was a kid, sometimes I would walk around for hours. You know...like when my mom and stepdad were fighting. I first just did it to get out of the house, not listen to all that noise. But then, I started liking it. My mind would just kinda...go. And I would have all these ideas."

"Yeah? What kind of ideas?"

Vayos is still squeezing Hectus's forearm. His grip has tightened. "Like, oh, what if there was a way you could order any movie right from your TV? I know they have that now. But I had the idea back then. I just didn't tell nobody. Maybe I should've. I could've gotten like a...what's it called? A paternal."

"Patent."

"Yeah, yeah. When I started working, I was so busy, you know, during the day, and after my shift, I was so tired. I didn't go for no more walks. I want to do it again. I'm gonna."

"I'll go with you." Hectus taps Vayos's hand, a signal for him to let go of his forearm. "You just hang here and get some rest. I'm going to take care of this problem for us."

34

Cole occupies the south wing's tight supply closet with Diaz, who sits on the floor with his back against metal shelves and a compression bandage around his sliced thigh. The giant chess piece he used as a cane to get here is jammed on a shelf between cardboard boxes. On the wall is a calendar from last year with various notes scribbled in the December date boxes.

Using tweezers from the first-aid kit, Cole removed from his gunshot wound bits of torn sleeve fabric, which could cause an infection. Since a forearm doesn't have as much mass as other body parts, the bullet passed through the flesh, which is good. However, a significant percentage of the muscle was ripped up. He wraps gauze around the tender skin.

"Looks like you know how to do that pretty well," Diaz says.

"Unfortunately not the first time I've been shot."

Diaz's head tilts toward his shoulder. "Why do you think we spent so many years over there?"

"A lot of reasons."

"How many of them benefited guys like me and you?"

Cole takes a compression bandage from the first-aid kit. "Do I think a lot of businesspeople got rich from contracts that came from those wars? Yeah. Do I think a few DC insiders who're friends with those businesspeople indirectly benefited because of those contracts? Probably."

Diaz nods, letting out a sarcastic chuckle. "Mm-hmm."

"But..." Cole says. "When we were over there, guys like us stopped a lot of terrorists planning to do bad things to good Americans." He wraps the bandage over his forearm. "You were a part of that. Don't ever forget it."

Diaz looks away with a pensive expression.

Though this supply closet is a decent place to hide, Cole will remain at a disadvantage if he doesn't get some shoes and a change of clothing. He waves bye. Diaz does, too. Though Diaz doesn't quite smile, the tension around his eyes has eased. This is the first time all night he doesn't look dejected.

With his rifle aimed ahead, Cole steps out of the supply closet and looks around for activity. None. He sprints to his room, also in the south wing, opens the door with his keycard, and pushes his dresser against the inside. With the desk, bed, and sofa, he forms a stack that reaches the far wall, barricading the door from the hallway.

Inching open the curtains, he peers into the storm. No Children of the Sun are out there. But if any surfaces, Cole will put a sniper round through his head. He rips off his soaked, bloody clothing and changes into the outfit from his overnight bag that he packed for tomorrow. Fresh underwear, socks, boots, jeans, tee shirt, and sweatshirt with the bulletproof vest on top. Even though getting out of the wet clothes is a help, his body still aches.

The bathtub with the TV looks inviting. The hot water would feel great. But Cole doesn't have time for anything like that.

He calls Shauna. "You all right?" she asks.

"Fine. You may have a bit more negotiating leverage. Their numbers are lower."

"What do you mean? Some of them left?"

"No."

She's silent for a while. "Oh. Ah. I see."

"This thing between them and me is about more than money, now. If they stick around, they're putting their lives at risk. If they surrender, tell them I'll stand down."

"Gemento's phone is off. But I can reach out to him through hostages in the ballroom we've been in contact with. Maybe he'll bite." She ends the call.

In about three minutes, she calls back. "No go. Gemento said he'd never surrender to a man like you. He wanted me to tell you that you're no better than a cop like me. Just another idiot enforcer who's exploited by the rich for protection."

"He sounds like a fun guy."

"FYI, not long ago, I got some other news that's a bit more encouraging. A colleague told me Gemento's son, William Junior, has been attending high school in Missoula, near his maternal grandparents' home. We're assuming he moved in with them."

"Really good news."

"They're not answering their phones, though. Probably on account of how late it is. A local patrol unit is on the way to the house to bang on the doors and windows until someone wakes up. Just lay low until then and hope this works. I know you've had a handle on these guys so far, but still...they're very dangerous and you're still heavily outnumbered. You don't know what new tricks they may throw at you. Your daughter deserves to meet you one day."

He hasn't discussed his personal life with her yet. The police must've done their research on him. Before he snuck up to the north wing, he hid all his social-media profiles. Prior, Shauna must've seen his Instagram post of Lacey holding her stomach. For the caption, he wrote the due date between two emojis, a girl's face and a heart.

Though he's chosen to put himself in plenty of life-or-death situations over the years, this is the first time the consequences of his decisions will affect a little girl. He still hasn't adjusted to his new, unexpected role as a father, despite his enthusiasm about it. When he's in battle, he tends to ignore caution. But Shauna is right. He needs to remind himself that he's responsible for a baby's future now.

He's been wondering how the group in the game room has been holding up and considered heading down there to rejoin them. But more terrorists could be after him by now. Leaving the safety in here for exposure in the hallway would be an unwise gamble. So, after the call, he just sits on the bed and waits.

35

The odors of puke and piss in the game room have gotten worse. Men and women who have controlled personas in the Stallos office are now vomiting and urinating in front of their coworkers with no apparent shame. Though Eagle wishes, of course, this ordeal never happened, this night has been quite a liberating experience.

Unwritten social rules have dictated so much of his behavior since childhood. For his tenth birthday, his parents' friends got him a present, and he forgot to mail them a thank-you card. He was grounded for two weeks. Tonight in the hotel, all social norms have evaporated. Yet, life has gone on.

Though Eagle grew up the son of a surgeon, and had plenty of advantages, he was still known as the pudgy, unathletic kid with the lisp. In sixth grade, he tried out for the basketball team at his prestigious private middle school. The coach slipped letters into the lockers of all the kids who were picked. A few guys who made the team played a prank on Eagle, giving him a letter, even though he was cut.

Beaming with pride, he showed up at the first practice. All the kids snickered as the coach pulled him aside and broke him the news. Holding back tears, Eagle screamed at them, "You all suck." Even though he'd made improvements on his lisp by then, his emotions were high and he botched the *s* in *suck*, causing the laughter to get even louder. He ran out of the gym and never played sports again.

He's still pudgy and unathletic with a slight lisp, and now, is on his way to being bald too. The unwritten rules say if a guy like him ever wanted to earn the respect of his male peers or date a beautiful woman, he needed to be a major success in business. Yale, Stallos Energy, a management position before thirty. He was on his way. Building a tech empire someday seemed doable.

But he could've had it all wrong. He doesn't even like tech stuff. Maybe another path out there is better for him. He isn't certain what, but when this night is over, and he goes back home, he's going to do some thinking.

A banging noise carries over from the front of the room. "Sammy," a middle-aged coworker says to him, his real name.

"Tonight, it's Eagle."

The coworker points at the room's door, rattling against the barricade. After Cole left, his right-hand man Eagle came to be viewed as the one in charge in here. His jacket is still off, plus his sleeves rolled up, part of the Dean Martin vibe he's adopted in the hope of relaxing the others. But a circle of sweat builds on his back as the hostages stare at him, as if waiting for him to do something.

He tries to imagine what Cole would do. Calm. Information. He'd keep calm and collect information before acting.

"Who, uh, who's there?" Eagle asks, toward the hallway.

No response. Hostages back away from the door while others hide behind the bar, the tables, the games.

"Probably just a hotel worker the terrorists missed," Eagle says. "Plenty of other places to hide. Not worth us opening the door."

In a moment, the door stops shaking. The tension in hostages' expressions fades a bit. Some return to the booze bottles they've been swigging from. Eagle sips a water. About five minutes pass.

Crrrack. Broken glass flies. One of the hallway benches bursts through the window. Two shrieking women scramble out of the way as it slides across the floor. The cold outside air rushes into the room, a few snowflakes mixed in.

Hostages backpedal from the window, a few tripping over each other. A terrorist on the other side of the broken glass aims a rifle at them. His three associates zip-tied to the shuffleboard table yell in celebration.

The man with the rifle slams the butt into the jagged opening in the window, widening it, then climbs inside. The only other gun in the room is the one that's been at Eagle's waist for a while. But he's never fired it, or any gun, ever.

"Hands up," the intruder screams at the crowd.

The hostages comply. Nobody tries to stand in his way as he marches toward his tied-up associates. The circle of sweat on Eagle's back grows. More seeps from his hairline. If this terrorist frees the others, their numerical advantage against Cole will steepen.

Thou shalt not kill. Another rule. But in the right context, a rule that should be broken.

Eagle pulls the Sig Sauer from his pants and fires at the intruder. He misses high, the bullet shattering a wall lamp. Hostages scream.

The terrorist appears startled, but just for a split-second. He looks around. His black sunglasses stop on the pudgy, unathletic, balding kid with the lisp pointing the pistol.

The terrorist's shoulders move, squaring his rifle to Eagle. However, before the guy takes a shot, Eagle takes a second.

He learned from his mistake. He aims a bit lower this time. The round pumps through the terrorist's neck. He stumbles back into the wall. One hand breaks off the rifle, which bobs from the other.

Eagle stomps toward him and fires again. This bullet hits his head. The rifle falls from his grip and he falls to the floor. Blood cascades from the two bullet holes in him. He doesn't move.

Except for Eagle's panting, the room is quiet for about ten seconds. Then one of his coworkers starts clapping. A second joins in. Then a third.

Soon, all the hostages give him a round of applause. He's been applauded before, like at school graduations, but this is the first time in his life people have cheered for him because of a physical act. Smiling, he tips a pretend hat to the crowd, like what baseball players do after a big home run.

Among the group, Eagle's eyes find Breann, the pretty coworker he's been too afraid to speak to. "Hey," he says.

She grins. "Hey."

36

Hectus jogs to the south wing. While patrolling the east, he heard a pair of gunshots, which sounded like pistol rounds, not from the rifle of his associate down there. Hectus tried him on the walkie-talkie, but has gotten no reply.

Through a window facing the southeast courtyard, he notices a massive hole in another window, the game room's. He takes the next exit door outside and stays tight to the building so nobody in the game room can see him coming. He curls his index finger around the trigger of his pistol.

The snow is gorgeous, he can't help but admit to himself, though he would never make a comment like that out loud. It's something a chick would say. The way the whiteness covers the hilly lawn reminds him of snow days in elementary school, when he and other kids would gather in a field with sleds. No teachers, no parents, for just a few hours, the children stood apart from the adult world and all its rigidity. Another thought enters his mind, Vayos's bloody, twitchy eyes. Hectus wonders if he will ever see anything gorgeous, like fresh snow, again.

Hectus will use a drill from the maintenance room on the thief's legs, just like the Iraqis did to him. He'll leave just enough strength in the man where he can hit the buttons on his phone to give back the crypto. Then Hectus will pry open his mouth and force the drill inside. He'll demolish his teeth, his gums, his tongue, just to make him feel the pain, then finish him off straight through the throat.

Just before the game-room window, Hectus removes his sunglasses for a brighter view and cranes his neck toward the glass. He peeks at a portion of the room and yanks his head back. At least one of his guys is on the floor, tied to some table. The hostages seem weary, some even drunk. However, the thief may be in there among them.

"It's me," Hectus shouts.

"Yo," a colleague calls back, excitement in his voice. "Get us the fuck out of here."

"What's the hostiles situation in there?"

"The ex-army guy who tied us up took off a while ago. All that's left is some chubby kid with a pistol. Five nine tops, like thirty, dark hair with a bunch of weird mousse or some shit in it. He just got one of us, though. So be alert."

The man who Hectus sent south just minutes ago must be gone. Hectus remembers how happy the guy was when he arrived in Montana from Akron, Ohio. Though he was more excited to reach Moldova, being around like-minded individuals in Montana improved his dreary life. At just nineteen, he attended a strike at the headquarters of where he worked. By accident, he knocked over a gate that hit some executive in the head. He was charged with manslaughter, a crime that put him in prison for years and hindered his future job endeavors.

If the ex-army thief left the chubby kid with a gun, he must trust him. The kid could know the thief's name. Hectus reaches into a pocket of his cargo pants, activates a military device known as a flash-bang, and tosses it through the hole in the window.

A moment later, a booming sound and blinding light explodes

out of it. Hectus jumps through the window, taking advantage of the crowd's flash-bang-induced disorientation. He spots the kid with the gun. He's hunched over, blinking.

Hectus pistol-whips him across the cheek. The kid topples to the floor and Hectus steps on his back and rips the gun from his hand. Some stiff in a tux scrambles for the rifle beside the corpse of the Children of the Sun member. Before the douche grabs the weapon, Hectus fires a bullet through his temple.

Though most of the crowd is still recovering from the flash-bang, some have regained enough vision to notice a new dead peer on the floor, a stream of blood leaking from his skull around a couple chunks of brain. A few hostages yell in terror, while others just stare.

Hectus zip-ties the dazed fat kid's wrists behind his back, pulls him to his feet, and cuts the binds off his three associates with his switchblade. One collects the rifle while the others describe what the ex-army thief looks like. They gathered that he's an outside construction worker, but never heard his name.

Hectus puts his sunglasses back on. "Let's get some information out of this one. We're all better off in the ballroom, with the curtains. Come on."

The Children of the Sun kick apart the barricade and drag the chubby kid into the corridor. No sign of the thief. At the intersection, Hectus trots east to Vayos, still on the bench, then puts his arm around him, guides him to the group, and they all continue north.

The brothers walk with pride in their gaits, even Vayos, who stumbles a bit. In possession of the fat kid, they're about to deliver a prize to Gemento, their venerated leader. Gemento has done so much for all these men. Though he never attended college, he has a large appetite for knowledge, which he's fed with self-education for decades. A brilliant man, he's never needed some professor to explain anything to him. He can see things not obvious to the typical person.

When Hectus started spending a lot of time on online forums, he was, of course, mad at the army, which abandoned him. But Gemento's astute blog posts showed him that the army was just one component of a much bigger system that's been engineered to keep most citizens enslaved in invisible shackles.

Other Children of the Sun had similar epiphanies when coming across Gemento's teachings. At first, many were irate at specific companies or institutions. Gemento helped them understand that a certain entity was not their problem. Instead, their problem was the small group of people who presided over every company and institution in America.

This group impoverishes others while enriching itself. Its mechanism of power extraction was designed to be complex on purpose, crossing through a multitude of political and economic channels, so average people wouldn't even notice it and wouldn't revolt against it. Most have no idea they're even being fucked. Gemento has inspired his followers to stand against this dark, powerful force.

Hectus concludes that he was a bit rash earlier, when becoming upset at his leader for not leaving the hotel while they still had the money. Hectus has a temper. But now he's feeling better and seeing clearer. Not only will they get back the crypto, but Rose and Hampton will confess, which will send a powerful message to the country. The Children of the Sun are engaged in the greatest fight of America's twenty-first century. If they win, they will be viewed as great men. Maybe not at first. But history will change that.

When Hectus opens the ballroom doors, the crowd gazes at the bruised party guest with them. A couple hostages say something about "Sammy."

Hectus shoves the kid onto the floor near Gemento, who eyes

his body and asks, "This fat piece of shit has been causing all that trouble?"

Hectus clarifies. Gemento shakes the hands of the three men who've been missing, thanking them for their bravery, then kneels beside the kid and rips the phone from his pocket. Hectus gazes at the screen. No passcode, Gemento gets right in and scans through recent calls and text messages. Nothing of value stands out. Any communication between the kid and the thief must've been in person.

"What's your friend's name?" Gemento asks.

"I don't know what you're talking about," the kid says.

Gemento kicks him in the nose. The bridge shifts half an inch to the side, the crack of bone audible. Blood sprays from his nostrils. He writhes in the puddle, groaning. A nearby woman cries.

"Let's try again," Gemento says. "What's his name?"

The treads of Hectus's muddy boot are imprinted onto the fat kid's back, which rises and falls as he huffs. "Like I said, I don't know what you're talking about."

Gemento turns to Hectus and laughs. Hectus pops open his switchblade and sticks the tip up a nostril of the kid's twisted nose.

"He's going to ask you again," Hectus says. "If you give him the same answer, I'm going to cut your nose off. Then make you eat it."

"What's his name?" Gemento asks.

The kid pants for a few moments. "Fine." He closes his eyes. "Conner."

"Last name?"

"I never got it."

"You work construction with him?"

"No. I'm in the compliance department. Look me up on

LinkedIn, Samuel Wibbons. I just met him tonight. I don't know anything about him but his first name."

Hectus does the search on LinkedIn. It checks out. He gives Gemento a nod.

Gemento lets out a long exhale. "Somebody must've invited him. Who?"

"I'm a new manager," the kid says, his voice a weird pitch from his battered nose. "This is the first time I ever got invited to this party. I have no idea how they get names on the list."

When the Children of the Sun planned tonight's operation, they didn't think the individual backgrounds of the Stallos employees would be of any importance, so never researched them. But that can change.

Hectus taps Gemento on the shoulder and nods away from the crowd. Once they walk out of earshot, Hectus points down at his phone and says, "This site, LinkedIn, it's got a page for the company. All these dirtbags have profiles attached to it with their names, photos, titles, job descriptions, all that shit. All we need do is go through them until we find someone who oversees construction. Then sink our teeth into whoever that happens to be until we get our answer."

37

Cole paces his hotel room, staring down at his phone, waiting for a callback from Shauna. At the end of the wing, near the game room, he heard some gunshots and what sounded like a flash-bang.

He's kept the lamp off, wanting to avoid light edging around the curtains and drawing attention from outside. The only light squeezes in from under the door. In the dark, the painting on the wall, of the sun setting over a mountain, looks like it's of just a circle and triangle.

His phone vibrates. He asks Shauna, "What is going on in the south wing?"

"We're getting reports from the inside that a hostage was beaten, and another is dead."

Cole sinks onto the bed with a heavy feeling in his stomach. The faces of all the people in the game room flash through his mind.

"Another terrorist is dead, too," she says. "But the three you tied up were freed."

The feeling in his stomach becomes even heavier. "The two hostages. You get names?"

The line goes silent for a few seconds. "The murdered one, Scott Zaddel. The beaten one, Samuel Wibbons."

"Eagle," Cole says, his voice tense.

"What?"

"Wibbons, it's what I call him. Why'd they go after him?"

"Brought him to the ballroom for questioning."

"About what?"

"You."

"What about me?"

"Your name."

The terrorists tried to subdue Cole with force, but were unsuccessful, so now seem to have altered their strategy. Just as he and Shauna wanted Gemento's real name for external leverage, Gemento could want Cole's for the same.

Cole let Eagle hold onto that pistol for safety. However, the gun must've made him a target, and now he's far from safe. Though Cole worries about his new friend, at least his family should be okay. Before he went to the north wing to take the crypto, he called the Timber Ridge PD and asked them to put a car in front of his cabin to monitor it until this is over. A second unit has been passing by his brother's place and his pop's.

Though his family leaving their houses and hiding out somewhere would be securer than an at-home police watch, Cole doesn't want to wake them at this late hour with an account of him squaring off against terrorists, Lacey in particular. Her stress-hormone levels would skyrocket, which could affect the baby's health.

"How bad is Eagle hurt?" Cole asks.

"Severely beaten is what I was told. But, despite the attack, he didn't give you up. Told them your name was Conner."

Cole is appreciative Eagle tried to protect him. However, lying to the terrorists has made Eagle's predicament even more menacing. Savvy Gemento would want to somehow verify the name given. If the truth comes out, the vindictive Children of the Sun won't forgive Eagle's deception. The beating he already received will become just the start of his problems. To avoid this, the terrorist takeover must end before Gemento learns Cole's real identity.

"Any progress on Gemento's son?" Cole asks.

"Still waiting to hear back from local PD. With the storm road closures, it could take a while for the car to get to the grandparents' house."

Another bleak update.

When Cole first entered this room earlier this evening, it exuded vitality. But barricaded inside in the darkness, he feels like he's in a solitary-confinement cell he can't leave. If he went up to the ballroom and tried to extract Eagle, the terrorists, now with three of their men back, would have plenty of opportunity to kill Cole, forcing his daughter to grow up without a dad.

He tries to think of a backup plan. However, at his disadvantageous position, the options range from bad to horrid.

38

Ollie needs a fucking cigarette. He's been so consumed by this terrorist shit, having a smoke hasn't occurred to him. But the stress has gotten so bad, his body is having an unignorable nicotine craving.

"You all right?" Rose asks, who must hear his teeth chattering.

"They asked Sammy about construction. Then one of them went on LinkedIn. Now all of them are on their phones, probably going through all of our profiles, looking for someone who deals with construction. Only a matter of time before they come across the executive project engineer and read my job description."

Rose nods. She seems to understand the gravity of Ollie's situation. He debates logging into LinkedIn and editing his profile, faking his job information. However, once the other employees in the room piece together that the terrorists are looking for a construction manager, to save themselves, at least one of them is certain to give up Ollie.

"It's better if I get ahead of this problem," he says to Rose.

"What are you considering?"

He puts his hand on her bare shoulder. It feels so good, he

feels guilty. "I...I might have an idea." He straightens his bow tie and approaches Gemento with careful steps.

The tall terrorist leader peers down at the shorter man through black lenses. Gemento is still, appearing like a statue.

"I think I can help you," Ollie says.

Gemento is still for another moment, then points at the corner with the instruments. Ollie joins him there, tripping over the bass. He glimpses Rose to make sure she wasn't watching, then says, "The guy you're looking for. I know who he is."

"You have his last name?"

"And his first. FYI, it ain't Conner."

Gemento looks over his shoulder at Sammy Wibbons, plopped on a chair, his hands still zip-tied, shreds of a cocktail napkin in his nostrils trying to stop the bleeding from his kicked-in nose. A female coworker in her fifties gives his arm a motherly stroke.

"Either the fat kid's lying to me or you are," Gemento says.

"Maybe the kid isn't lying, just heard the name wrong. He only met him tonight and—"

"He's bullshitting me or you are. You trying to tell me someone happened to hear a name wrong feels manipulative. You're not off to a great start convincing me you're the honest one."

"Look, I...I'm not going to speak for Sammy. All I can tell you is I personally work with the guy you're after. And I'm positive of his name."

"Wonderful. What is it?"

"I want something in return."

Gemento smirks. "What you'll get in return is me not snapping the bones in your fingers until you give me the information."

"I'm going to give it. All I'm asking for is a little something as a thank-you."

"The name, before I lose my patience."

"The guy you're looking for is engaged. And she's pregnant,

FROZEN DREAM

to boot. I'm assuming you've got more men in your...organization, whatever you call this...who aren't in the hotel. You get a couple of them to stop by the house. Their presence alone should do the trick. He'll give you back the money if your men leave his woman alone. All you need is his address. I was just there last week. I can give it to you right now."

"And what is it you want in exchange?"

Ollie pulls his Marlboros and lighter from his tux jacket and sparks one. The warm smoke is therapeutic. "You don't like the governor. Guess what? I don't like him either. He's a trust-fund pansy who never worked a real job in his life. Me, I came from nothing. Anything I have today was from busting my ass. You want Hampton to make an admission on camera, so be it." Ollie blows smoke from his nose. "But I'm somewhat of a confidante of Rose's. We don't keep secrets. I know how things with the pipeline went down. You should give her a pass."

"What they did wound up depressing my wife to the point of me losing her. Hampton and Rose killed her. Both of them will pay."

"She feels terrible about what happened. It was Hampton's idea, not hers. His reelection campaign was based on the economy. Getting the project approved gave him street cred. He hired the guys who put the fertilizer in your water. Not Rose. All she's guilty of is staying silent."

This is a lie. In reality, Hampton, Rose, and Ollie were all responsible. Stallos Energy approached Gemento, AKA William Laud, to extend the pipeline over his land, which was in a crucial position along a pathway free of tribal and environmental concerns. However, Laud, the proud proprietor of a fifth-generation family business, refused to let outsiders build on his farm. To help Rose secure the deal, Ollie offered an alternative solution. With his engineering background, he knew the right quantities and methods for tainting Laud Farm's water.

One night, he dressed up in a black outfit and a mask, somewhat similar to what's on Gemento, and did what needed to be done. Hampton, who oversees the Department of Environmental Quality, had it pummel Laud with enough fines to force him to sell. The farm was purchased by a shell corporation controlled by investors in Stallos Energy, who stood to profit a sizable sum from the pipeline approval.

"You're her confidante, huh?" Gemento asks. "You sleeping with her?"

Just the mention of that excites Ollie. Then, reality sets back in. "No, it's nothing like that."

"I'm not honoring any deal with you unless I know your information is accurate." Gemento points at Sammy. "If I find out you're the one telling the truth, that fat kid is getting a bullet in his head. If I find out he's the one telling the truth, you are. The guy, what's his name?"

Ollie takes a long drag of his cigarette. "Cole Maddox."

39

On his new burner phone, a spare taken from a gear bag, Gemento speaks to a Children of the Sun member who didn't come to the Alpine Grand tonight. Less than half the group volunteered for the dangerous task of invading the hotel, with the rest available for support from the outside. Gemento relays the home address that Ollie provided for Cole Maddox. The guy on the line and an associate will head to Timber Ridge ASAP to confirm the information and act on it.

A few moments after the call is over, another comes in, from the woman cop. He says, "I appreciate your persistence, Officer, but unless you're calling to tell me your man on the inside has decided to give back all of the money he stole from me, I have no reason to speak with you."

"I'm not calling to speak with you. But someone else would like to. Hold for a moment while I put him through."

The line is silent for a few seconds. Then, a voice says, "Dad?"

Gemento's stomach drops. He hasn't heard this voice in months. "Will."

"The cops at grandma and grandpa's showed me a video of a

woman getting shot. You couldn't tell who did it with the mask, but they said it was you. I told them no. That you'd never do anything like that. Right? Right, Dad?"

The boy is still young. He doesn't understand the difficult things adults sometimes need to do in the name of what's right. "How have you been?" is all Gemento can come up with as a reply.

Will Jr. lets out a noise that sounds like a put-on laugh. "I'm only calling because the cops made me."

"They're part of the problem. We need—"

"They told me to ask you to stop. Stop whatever it is you're involved in tonight. I don't know what exactly it is. But, from what they told me, it sounds nuts. Absolutely mental. And it seems best if you would just stop."

"I'm going to make the people responsible tell the truth tonight. There will be another video. You're going to finally see that I didn't screw up on our farm and get fertilizer in our own water. You're going to finally see that everything that happened wasn't my fault. That it was their fault. I'll find a way to reach out to you and give you my new address. If you'd like to join me, I'd love to have you. If you just wanted to visit, that would be...that would be really nice, too."

"I'm happy at Grandma and Grandpa's."

"Yeah. I'm sure. They're good people. And I know they love you. But if you, you know, if you change your mind, then...the offer is open. Open-ended."

Another voice comes through the line, whispering. A cop must be over Will Jr.'s shoulder, giving him instructions on how to sabotage his dad.

"Can you please let the hostages go?" Will Jr. asks.

"If I did that, the people who started all of this won't tell you the truth about them pouring fertilizer—"

"Enough about the fertilizer. Fine, you weren't responsible for it getting in the water. Fine, I believe you. Great. There. Can you let the hostages go now?"

"I was the victim in all this. You finally see that now?"

"It was never about the fucking fertilizer," the boy shouts.

Gemento waits a moment, giving his son a chance to calm down, then says, "None of this would've happened if my water wasn't poisoned and my land wasn't stolen."

"It wasn't about you losing the farm. When Mom was still...I tried to tell you this back then. But you wouldn't listen. You were too in your own head, off in Grandma and Grandpa's basement on the computer, doing whatever it was you were doing, running your weird anti-American message boards or—"

"Hardworking small-business owners built this country. But the people in charge of it no longer look at us like partners. They look at us like obstacles that need to be squashed. America having millions of independent, strong small businesses is a threat to them. Instead, they'd rather if the economy was consolidated into just a few mega-corporations. With their friends on the boards. A few big companies are easier to control than many small ones. That's where this country is headed. You need to open—"

"If you wanted to change things, you should've run for office. Not done something like—"

"Oh, Son. A concerned citizen can't just run for office and expect to get anywhere. You need the blessing of the power structure. Funding, media access, voter analytics. They won't give these tools to someone who's looking to burn down the system they're on top of."

"If not run for office, then, I don't know, protest or something. Not this. Do you even have a better system in mind? Or is all this just about burning down the existing one because it screwed you over?"

Gemento sits on a chair. "It screwed you over too, Will. Taking over the farm one day was your birthright."

"You're right. I was upset about us losing the farm. So was Mom. We needed you. But you wouldn't even be around us, other than to eat dinner. Then it was back to the basement to chat online with a bunch of wackos about some American dystopia."

"I had an obligation to let other people know what happened to us, and what might happen to them. We're not the only ones who were hurt by this sort of corruption. I connected with men who were on the verge of suicide, and—"

"And what, you saved their lives?"

"Yes."

"Their lives were more important than Mom's, huh?"

"She was black-out drunk. She shouldn't have been driving. How was I supposed to—"

"Why was she blacked out that night? Why was she blacked out almost every night for two months leading up to that night?"

"Because they took everything from us," Gemento yells.

"You're one of the smartest people I've ever met. But you still couldn't see it then. And you still can't see it now. What she wanted was so simple."

A vein on Gemento's temple pulses.

"You lost your farm," Will Jr. says. "But you acted like you lost everything. You'd go down to the basement and post online like it was the end of the world. But you still had her. You still had me. All she wanted you to do was act like you still had something."

Gemento's vein pulses harder. When he looks at photos of his wife, he feels joy for the memories, but also a vague sense of guilt. But now, it no longer is vague. As hard as the realization is to accept, his son is correct. After Gemento was forced to move into his in-laws' house, he did avoid his family. But not because he didn't love them. He loved them so much that, for letting them down, he felt an unbearable discomfort in their presence. But that must've just been shame. The guilt came after she died.

"Dad, are you there?" Will Jr. asks, after a long silence.

"I still have you, and you still mean everything to me."

"Did you shoot that woman at the hotel?"

Gemento takes a deep breath. "I have to go now."

"Jesus, you did. Can you free the hostages at least, and make this—"

"This is about more than me. I have men depending on me. I really have to go now."

"Wait, you—"

Gemento ends the call.

40

Cole gazes at the large black TV in his room, its shape faint in the darkness. The wind squeals outside the window. "Beaten severely" is how Shauna described Eagle's state. The kid must be in agony. All because of Cole. If he didn't give him that pistol, Eagle wouldn't have been targeted. If Cole left the safety of this room to reunite with the others in the game room, he could've warded off the assault, preventing Eagle's capture.

Shauna calls. Cole, expecting news about William Jr.'s conversation with his father, asks, "Did it work?"

"No."

He closes his eyes and lets out a long exhale.

"I know this is bad," she says. "But there is one more thing we can do. Because of you, the Children of the Sun are all congregated in the ballroom, hesitant to venture out. That may stop you from killing more of them, but does enable something else."

"What?"

"The curtains in the ballroom prevent our snipers from seeing in, but also prevent the Children of the Sun from seeing out. If we flew over another drone, they likely wouldn't spot it."

"The only reason that plan was doable before was because one of their guys came outside to walk a path around the bombs. If they're all hunkered down in the ballroom, that's not happening."

"Different kind of drone. The FBI is equipping this one with bomb sensors. Apparently, if it flies low enough, these sensors could pick up the location of the bombs, even through feet of snow."

"I like the idea of a bomb-sensing drone. What I don't like is the timing. The FBI needs to assemble the thing, drive it over here through the storm, then fly it all over acres of hotel property."

"Four hours. If the explosives get mapped and SWAT gets up there, this can all be over by morning, which isn't—"

"More hostages are on track to get slaughtered over the next four hours. Any minute now, they can find out Eagle lied about me being Conner. They'll kill him, and keep killing a hostage every hour Rose Stallos and Grant Hampton don't confess. Four hours can mean five more murders."

"The last thing I want is to see that. But this is a very complex situation, with well over a hundred lives at stake. If we can end it in four hours, and get the vast majority of people in there out in one piece, I would consider this a win. A win you should be proud of, more than anyone."

"This won't be a win for me if Eagle is murdered. He doesn't have any training on how to handle an interrogation, but he stepped up, took a beating for me, and didn't cave. I'm pulling him out of there."

"Going into that ballroom by yourself is a suicide mission. I know this is tough, Cole. But you're going to have to stop thinking about this guy Eagle."

"I don't have to do this by myself."

"Someone in there is capable of assisting?"

"There's an ex-Marine security guard, but his leg is too

messed up. He can help me out in another way, though. But we're also going to need support from your end."

"From out here, in the ballroom? What? How?"

"I'll explain. I put together a backup plan."

"That's fantastic."

"Not really. It was a backup plan for a reason."

41

Shauna watches the wild snow from under the police tent, thinking about the call she just had with Cole. The heavy wind blows a clump of flakes into the shape of a diamond. They remain suspended that way for a split second, then explode apart.

After a minute or so of deliberation, she calls Ed Rowack, the SWAT commander of the helicopter unit that never took off. She's met him once. A nice man with thick red hair and five kids. In his free time, Rowack and his wife run a small YouTube channel giving DIY home-improvement tips. Shauna used one of them to fix a shower curtain.

"Hey," Rowack says.

"How quickly can you guys get over here?"

"My whole team is still on standby with the grounded bird. Ten and a half miles away. Might be a rocky ride with the weather, but my pilot can cover that distance pretty quickly. What happened? You found out the terrorists were bluffing about the RPG?"

"We have no reason to believe that was a bluff. All the threats they've made tonight, they've acted on."

"What then? You guys figured out where the bombs are and

want us to assist on the ground? I heard something about an FBI bomb-sensing plan, but the ETA was a lot longer than—"

"No. We still don't know where the bombs are."

"Well, if it's still too dangerous to get inside by land or air, what do you expect us to do? Last I checked, no sea in Bozeman."

"Our guy on the inside, Maddox, he wanted me to pass a suggestion to you."

"All right."

"He wants you to come in by air."

"Didn't you just say they almost definitely have a weapon capable of blasting us out of the air?"

"Yes."

Rowack lets out a sarcastic chuckle. "I knew Delta Force operated outside the box, but not outside the laws of reality."

"Again, what I'm about to tell you is only a suggestion. It's...risky, to say the least. And if you don't want to do it, I'd understand. But at this point, this is our last option to end this without more hostage deaths."

"Son of a bitch. Give me the broad strokes."

"If you guys flew over in the chopper, the noise should get the terrorists' attention. One of them is going to hustle outside to shoot you out of the air. In the meantime, Maddox is going to try to figure out the highest-probability place on the property where they're stashing the RPG. Then he's going to put himself in position for a rifle shot, lined up to the nearest exit. It should take the terrorist a few seconds to aim that big weapon and fire. Maddox will have a brief opportunity to put a bullet through his head before the RPG goes off."

"To save a few hostages, I'd be risking the lives of everyone on my team."

"Yes, but it could work. With the RPG shooter out of the picture, your pilot could safely hover over the roof. You guys could come down with rope ladders, break the windows, toss in tear gas, and swing inside."

"I heard there are a hundred twenty-one civilians in that ballroom. Once we're inside, who knows how many could get shredded up in a crossfire? We could lose more than we'd be saving."

"You'll be in gas masks and body armor, not the terrorists. They brought a few rifles with them, but you'd have more. You'd have an evident advantage. These men are unhinged, but not suicidal. If so, they would've strapped their bombs to their chests, not hidden them under the snow. Our hope is they surrender as soon as they see you guys. With no shots fired."

"That's all assuming we even get inside alive. Maddox can miscalculate where the RPG is and set up by the wrong exit door, forcing me and my guys to try to take out the terrorist who runs outside. We'd have to hit a ground target from a moving helicopter, in a ridiculously short time frame, in a blizzard. If this is going to work, we need Maddox to connect on his shot."

"I'm still waiting on him to give me his presumed location of the RPG. But unless he sees the weapon with his own eyes, which I doubt, you're not going to be operating on one hundred percent certainty. There's a reason this was the backup plan."

Rowack goes silent. She wonders if he's considering what Cole asked him to do, or considering whether Cole is insane.

42

Cole digs through carboard boxes on the shelves in the supply closet, looking for a pen. He just explained the RPG plan to Diaz, who watches on from the floor, his ripped-up leg extended. Cole sweeps his arm through a box of spare landline telephones, their plastic bodies clattering. Some objects slide around the bottom of the box. A computer mouse, a few AAA batteries, then, a pen.

Cole hasn't seen any paper and, instead of wasting valuable time looking for some, rips a side off the carboard box. He hands it and the pen to Diaz, who knows the architecture of the hotel and begins drawing a rough diagram.

"The cops tell me the first exterior security camera was blacked out at seven twelve PM," Cole says. "There's no video of the terrorists doing anything outside but walking up to some cameras with spray paint. According to the timing of nine-one-one texts from the ballroom, it looks like it wasn't invaded until seven fifty-eight. Disabling surveillance must've been their first order of business. Camera three went dark before any other."

Diaz points with the pen at his cross-shaped building drawing.

"Camera three is on this wall. They must've come in from the northeast."

"Even though the drone plan with the governor was a bust, the cops were still able to get some aerial footage. They didn't see any cars parked on the property that weren't already there. And patrol units haven't found any parked cars on the surrounding roads, so—"

"The terrorists must've gotten dropped off by friendlies, then came to the hotel through the woods, on foot."

"Without a vehicle to stash the RPG in, it must be somewhere inside."

"One of those pricks got me outside by pretending he was hurt. There's a third guard who's still unaccounted for. They must've taken him out, too. Not to mention, they planted all the bombs. A lot to do. And an RPG is pretty big, over three feet long and like twenty pounds. I'm sure they had plenty of other gear, too."

"They weren't going to slow themselves down by lugging around clunky gear bags. One of them must've been responsible for bringing that stuff inside as soon as they showed up."

"There are three side doors facing the northeast of the property. But you need an active-guest keycard to use any, which would've been tough to get during a private event. I'm sure they could've forced their way in somehow, but why waste time on that? One door in the building is wide open to the public twenty-four hours a day."

"A guy walking through the front door syncs with the cops' timeline. A series of interior cameras were blacked out, too, but the lobby one was the first to go."

"They obviously found out details about the party schedule, must've known everyone checked in by the time they arrived. The lobby would've been empty besides Leah, the front-desk girl on shift tonight."

"So Leah is at her desk and sees a masked man walk in and spray-paint a camera. What happens next?"

"She screams."

"Which nobody in the ballroom must've heard, with the band. Then she runs. The terrorist catches up to her. If he shot her, they would've heard that above the music, meaning—"

"She must be zip-tied. He must've dragged her into one of the rooms off the lobby, or else you would've seen her when you were up there before. Then he goes back outside, grabs the gear, and stashes it. The luggage room is closest to Leah's desk. The RPG might be in there with her."

"It's possible. But if their stronghold for the night was going to be the ballroom, wouldn't you think they'd want easy access to all their weapons from it? A luggage area by the front desk is a pretty far walk." Cole takes a deep breath. "But none of the hostages inside the ballroom reported seeing bags of equipment in there."

"Right behind the ballroom is the biggest kitchen on the whole property. Plenty of space to store things out of sight."

Cole nods. "The guy with the RPG comes in through the front and ties up Leah, who's probably in the luggage area. Then he somehow gets from the lobby into the kitchen behind the ballroom. If he walked directly through the party with gear bags, someone would've noticed. But walking through the hallways to the kitchen from the back probably would've gotten him spotted too. Guests were still trickling out of their rooms then."

"The basement." Diaz points at a spot on the lobby portion of the diagram. "There's a staircase here that brings you down there. A subterranean passageway cuts right under the ballroom. The guy with the gear takes that, which comes up on the other side of the ballroom. He could've peeked out the door, waited for the coast to be clear, then made the short walk right into the kitchen."

"And once he's back there, he opens up a door to the outside, letting in the rest of the terrorists, who black out the camera and take the cooks, and any other employees in there, hostage."

"That's it."

Cole pats him on the back. Diaz grins. His light-brown complexion has paled from blood loss, yet his eyes are full of life.

"So it's fair to say the RPG is highly likely right behind the ballroom," Cole says. "If the terrorists hear a chopper coming, and one of them goes back there to grab the weapon, where's the exit outside?"

Diaz closes his eyes as if trying to visualize the kitchen. "There are two external doors in the storage part of the kitchen, for deliveries. One facing east, the other west. Other than where they're pointing, they're indistinguishable from each other. It's anyone's guess which one the guy would run out of."

Cole was hoping for a single door. Fifty-fifty odds are horrendous, a life-or-death coin flip for a chopper full of cops. Rowack, the SWAT commander, suggested they keep the helicopter high upon arrival. If something went wrong and the terrorists got an RPG shot off, a high target would be hard to hit.

However, with these fifty-fifty odds of an east or west exit, the helicopter's noise must sway the RPG shooter one way over the other. The chopper will have to come from the side and get close enough to generate a distinct noise in that direction. It will have to make itself a much easier target.

Cole calls Shauna and tells her the lackluster news. She says she'll run the update by Rowack, but doubts he'll agree to a plan that's become even more dangerous than the original.

Once the call ends, Diaz reaches to the keys on his waist and says, "Hey, I have something for you." He removes a two-inch metal item from the keyring and hands it to Cole. It's a silver surfboard, with a vertical red line down the middle, the paint faded a bit. "That surfboard is good luck, man. Keep it on you when you go back out there. Consider it a gift for saving me from freezing to death."

Cole gazes at it, then puts it in his pocket. He doesn't believe in good-luck charms, yet appreciates the gesture. "You a surfer?"

"My dad taught me when I was young. That little surfboard was originally his, on a keychain he bought not long after he got to America. He gave it to me, to keep me safe, right before I shipped out to Iraq."

"Huh."

"Before he came to the US, he'd work sixteen hours a day and barely earn enough to feed himself. A wife and kids was out of the question. So he saved up everything he had to travel to Texas. A friend from his old town found him a job in Oklahoma. He liked it, but eventually wanted to make it to California. When he was a kid, he'd listen to The Beach Boys records. That whole sunny California thing seemed too good to even be true, like a dream."

Cole smiles. "It is a beautiful state."

"He found the keychain in a drugstore in Oklahoma. It was a promise he made to himself to eventually get to California and surf, just like The Beach Boys."

"And he did, huh?"

"But first, the Vietnam War happened. Even though he was only an American for a couple years, he volunteered to fight. He brought the surfboard to the jungle with him. Kept it in his fatigues the whole time. And he came back alive. When the war was over, he went right to California and bought a real, full-sized board. No lessons, nothing like that. Just got out in the water and tried teaching himself. He met my mom on that trip. He stayed there for the rest of his life."

"Thank you for giving this to me. But it's a family heirloom. I can't keep it."

"At least keep it on you tonight, until this is all over."

Cole nods. However, he is still unsure when this will be over. And worse, whether it will end in more bloodshed. He checks his phone. Still no word from Shauna on whether Rowack's team is flying over for support.

43

Arms crossed, Gemento stares at Ollie for a second, then at the fat kid, still seated with bloody napkin shreds up his nostrils. Gemento keeps looking back and forth between them, their frightened eyes watching him.

"We know who the liar is," Hectus says, appearing at Gemento's side.

They did a search for *Cole Maddox* on all the major social networks, but nothing came up. If the thief has profiles, he could've hidden them tonight in anticipation. But now, Hectus shows Gemento a picture on his phone of a dirty-blond teenager, from a page in a physical yearbook. They asked Ollie where the thief attended high school, and were informed that he went to the public one in Timber Ridge. So they told the two Children of the Sun sent there to break into the high school library and snatch the yearbook from the graduation year Ollie gave.

"Is that the son of a bitch?" Gemento asks.

"I just showed the picture to our men from the game room and they said that's the guy, just younger. Cole Maddox it is. Ollie was telling the truth."

"And the fat kid was lying."

Hectus grins, as if eager to administer the requisite punishment. Gemento wouldn't mind killing Ollie, too. That skinny little weasel may have told the truth about Cole Maddox, but not Rose Stallos. That slut had to have been involved in the fertilizer scam to a high degree. So Gemento lied, too, agreeing to Ollie's deal to spare her a public confession.

Gemento paces toward the fat kid. At the edge of Gemento's vision, the chandelier twinkles. It makes him recall his old life. He used to wake up early, 4:29 AM. When his parents were alive and lived in the farmhouse, his father got up at 4:30 every day. Setting the alarm just a minute earlier reminded Gemento that if he wanted the family business to grow under his leadership, he'd have to work even harder than his dad.

Before going out to the fields to join the crew, he'd head downstairs, make coffee, and gaze out the window. The sky would still be dark, yet with a glimmer of light, the promise of a new sun. With Ella and Will Jr. still asleep at that hour, the house would be quiet. Sometimes their dog, an Airedale terrier named Miles, would join him. Miles must've been able to sense Gemento appreciated the quiet at that hour, so would sit hushed at the base of his counter stool. Gemento did a lot of thinking during those cups of coffee.

He'd, of course, think about his crops, and about business decisions that needed to be made. But he'd spend more time on his family.

He liked to surprise Ella. Not with expensive gifts like jewelry. She didn't care much for things like that. Once, when they were out to dinner, a local female folk singer was performing on the restaurant's patio. Ella loved the music. When she went to the bathroom, Gemento got the singer's information and hired her to play on the farm for Ella's fortieth birthday, that summer. The performer did an acoustic cover of their wedding song, "Beast of Burden," by the Rolling Stones, that made Ella cry a little as they danced together under the string lights.

Will Jr. was into technology. He had all sorts of ideas for computer programs and machines that could make the farm more efficient. He's smarter than his dad. In the mornings, Gemento would read up on his laptop about tech stuff so he could have productive conversations with his son. Will Jr. was working on some scheduling program for the crops. Then the news came in about the poisoned water, distracting the whole family. The program was never finished.

Gemento approaches the fat kid, who springs off his chair and tries to run. But Hectus sprints up to him and trips him. His hands still zip-tied behind his back, the kid can't brace his fall, landing on his already-injured face. A bloody piece of a napkin flies out of a nostril. Hectus plants his boot on his back, on top of the imprint already there. The kid tries to break free, but can't.

Gemento pulls his pistol out of his holster. Hostages scramble away from him. "This young man lied to us," Gemento announces to the room. "For that, he will pay with his life." He peers at Rose and the governor, off by a wall. "After he dies, these two will have an hour to admit their own lies on video. If they don't, another one of you people will be killed. Actually...let's make it a half hour. And this will continue every half hour, until they do the right thing."

"Just fucking say what he wants," a freckle-faced female hostage screams at Rose and the governor. "You're going to really let us keep dying?"

"Say it, or I'll be the one who kills you," a mustached male hostage shouts. He hurls a wine glass at Rose and the governor. Shrieking, she ducks. The glass shatters against the wall, the wine from it splashing across the governor's chest.

Gemento smirks. He likes this. The fat kid hasn't stopped trying to free himself, sweating and wheezing. Gemento aims his gun down at the kid's head, right at the bald spot. Just as he's about to blow his brains all over the rug, he hears something outside.

Thunt, thunt, thunt. A whirring noise. Others in the room seem to notice it too, looking toward the windows. The noise gets louder. Then much louder. Heads turn to the window facing east.

Gemento dashes to it and inches back the curtain. A fucking helicopter. His heartbeat surges. The legs of armed men in tactical outfits hang out of the helicopter's open sides.

"SWAT," he yells.

He looks over his shoulder at his crew. They prepared for this. Hectus starts pointing around the room, giving orders. Two Children of the Sun guard the main ballroom doors, while others dart through the swinging doors at the back of the room. Gemento follows them into the kitchen.

In the service area, they pass trays of soggy salad that were never served. Heat lamps shine down on an empty table that never received appetizers from the oven. They continue to the food-storage area, where their gear waits.

Gemento yanks the zipper of a duffel bag, while the man who's been training with the RPG picks up another bag, containing the weapon and three rockets. He jogs to the exit door facing east and kicks it. The door moves just a few inches, then closes. He kicks it again. Same result. He pushes his hip against it and peers at the crease between it and its frame.

"Shit," he mutters. "A fucking tree branch fell. It's blocking it."

"Hotel front door," Hectus shouts. "The next quickest way to get outside from here with a clear shot to the east."

The guy nods and races out of the kitchen.

44

Cole kneels in an east-wing corridor, aiming his rifle through a window at the exterior food-delivery door that faces him. A moment ago, through the scope, he noticed the door open a bit and close a few times. Assessing the surrounding area, he sees something peeking out of the snow piled at the door's base. The end of a tree branch.

This isn't good.

Thunt, thunt, thunt. The SWAT chopper hovers. The RPG operator can pop out of the hotel in another spot, within moments. If Cole doesn't fix this problem, the five men in the helicopter are dead.

Cole sprints to the hallway intersection. If a tree branch is blocking the eastern food-delivery door, the western one would, of course, be an alternative, but the building would be obstructing a shot at the helicopter. The terrorist's closest exit for a viable shot would be the hotel's front door.

Cole runs toward it, despite the terrorist's head start from the kitchen. When Cole reaches the north wing, he sees a masked man at the other end of the long corridor, in the lobby, with a big bag. A split second later, just before Cole aims his rifle, the guy is gone, out the front door. Cole dashes into the conference room beside the ballroom. The lights off, the surface of the shiny, lacquered-wood table looks like the still water of a lake at night.

He whacks the eastern-facing window with the butt of his rifle, splintering it, then launches a chair through the cracked glass. He ducks for cover, just in case it happens to land on a bomb.

He juts his upper body through the broken window, the snow streaming down the collar of his sweatshirt. The terrorist stands on the northeastern lawn, an opened duffel bag at his feet, the RPG in one hand, a rocket the other.

Cole aims his rifle. But the terrorist seems to notice, diving under the bullet, into the snow. He lets go of the RPG, plus rocket, for a pistol at his waist and returns fire. Cole straightens his back, pulling his upper body into the conference room, avoiding a hit. But the round nails the window's edge, flinging glass at Cole's face. Pain fills his right eye. It waters. A piece of glass must've sliced it.

His vision blurs. He blinks a few times and fires a cover shot. When he inches his head outside, the terrorist isn't in sight. But his footprints in the snow are. They lead behind a boulder in the lawn. He didn't waste time picking up the RPG, but it's far closer to him than Cole.

The SWAT team must see what's happening. Bullets stream from the chopper into the boulder and the snow around it. However, the crouching terrorist stays guarded. The cops remain at a distance, as if hesitant to approach, in case he picks the RPG back up.

Cole could get a clear angle on the terrorist for a shot, but he'll need to go out into the lawn, where he'll be susceptible to hidden bombs, triggered at just ten pounds of weight.

He runs into the hallway. When he reaches the lobby, the clarity of his cut right eye is down to about seventy-five percent.

The stylized top of the *A* of the *AG* logo on the front desk is no longer even noticeable. He lowers his rifle to the edge of the main doorway, in a horizontal position. He lunges outside, pushing the gun along the ground. If an explosive were in his path, the rifle would clink its side. The light impact would be enough for him to know something is under the snow, yet not enough for a detonation.

He deepens into the lawn with his feet close together, within the rifle's width. In this odd, arched position, the pain in his wounded forearm is aggravated. The boulder comes into view. But the RPG, rocket, and terrorist don't. The guy must've snagged the items, avoided the SWAT rounds, and hid back behind the big rock. The chopper has turned around, as if to flee. However, it's still within striking range.

Keeping quiet, below the noise of the helicopter blades, Cole veers to the boulder's side. The back end of the RPG appears. The terrorist seems to be kneeling, aiming the weapon upward at the cops, his rear boot edging out from behind the rock.

Cole fires his rifle at the foot. The terrorist falls over, yelling. He lets go of the RPG. Part of his head becomes exposed. He rolls in the snow, aiming his pistol, but before he can squeeze the trigger, Cole puts a round through the top of his head. Blood sprays the snow-covered boulder in a shape that resembles an open hand.

Cole drags his rifle across the ground until he reaches the cover of the rock, then texts Shauna:

Clear.

45

Gemento's arm is wrapped around the neck of a hostage, the quivering woman serving as a human shield in anticipation of the SWAT team. She's been mumbling a prayer under her breath. Outside, he heard guns, but not an RPG. And he still hears those damn chopper blades. That meddling motherfucker Cole Maddox must've had something to do with this.

Despite the defensive precautions the Children of the Sun took tonight, a police raid was a possibility. But Gemento accounted for it, bringing gas masks, which he and the other Children of the Sun wear. Blinded Vayos sits out of harm's reach in the service area, while Gemento is in the ballroom with the other four active men, each clutching a gun and a female hostage.

The helicopter noise gets even louder. It seems to be hovering right over the ballroom. Soon, a high-pitched sound rings out. Shards of broken glass spurt from between two closed curtains to the east. A pointy metal object on a chain, which looks like a boat anchor, swings into the ballroom for a moment, then pendulums out of sight. A few moments later, the object crashes through a window to the west.

A tear-gas canister flies through each broken window. They

plummet over two stories, clinging on impact. Hostages scurry out of the way as the canisters skip across the floor, white smoke billowing out. People begin coughing. Some clench their eyelids and stick their hands over their mouths. Others crumple to their knees.

The young woman Gemento has headlocked groans. She tries to say something, but the gas overwhelms her, the words inaudible. As she coughs, her throat jerks against his bicep. A couple more canisters zip into the room. The debilitating effect on the hostages intensifies. But, in their masks, Gemento and his brothers remain unfazed.

Soon, the high-ceilinged room is filled with a white haze resembling the snowstorm outside, the glow of the chandelier dimmed. The knees of the woman in Gemento's grasp weaken. He tugs her upward. Saliva spews from her mouth onto his sleeve.

A man in black tactical gear soars through the eastern window on a rope, boots first. More broken glass scatters the floor. He's in a helmet, mask, and heavy body armor, *POLICE* across his chest. A second cop busts in from the western window. Then another to the east and another to the west. The four SWAT officers spread out into the four corners of the room. Each points an assault rifle at a nearby Children of the Sun member.

"Drop your guns," a cop shouts, his mask muffling his voice a bit.

"Drop yours," Gemento shouts back. The cops must've thought this would be an easy fight, not accounting for Gemento being smart enough to defend against tear gas.

The room goes silent for a while besides agonized coughing from hostages. In the white haze, their silhouettes thrash.

"Your RPG isn't a threat anymore," the cop says. "My pilot is going to keep picking up more police and dropping us off. There'll be a lot more of us than you, soon."

"But not now."

The room again quiets.

"There's more of us than anyone," a male voice screams. Gemento looks toward it. The fat kid. His hands are still zip-tied behind his back, but he's on his feet. He coughs a couple times and yells at the crowd, "We outnumber these assholes more than ten to one. Let's quit listening to what they tell us to do and get out of this damn room." He sprints toward the main ballroom doors, his belly bouncing.

He seems to have motivated others. Three more men rush toward the doors. Four others, and two women, join them. The Children of the Sun member by the exit appears antsy, backpedaling. He slams a guy in the gut with the butt of his rifle. The hostage falls to the floor, but the others keep coming. The fat kid steps on a chair and leaps off it. He drop-kicks the Children of the Sun member in the head. Both guys and the human shield topple. She and the fat kid get up, but the Children of the Sun member stays on a knee, dazed. People brush past him.

A hostage tears open the doors and over a dozen flee into the north-wing hallway. Their brazenness seems to motivate even more of their peers, who charge toward the exit. Another Children of the Sun member tries to stop them, but struggles, losing control of his human shield. As he scurries out of the way of the stampede, a SWAT officer pumps a bullet through his gas mask. He drops to the rug, dead.

Gemento's skin heats from stress. His crew now has even numbers with the cops. If human shields become too difficult to hang onto, the better-equipped cops would have an advantage in a shootout. Gemento must alter course.

"Go out with them," he screams, pointing toward the exit.

Dragging his human shield, he joins the stampede. Other Children of the Sun do the same. The police chase them, however, among a disarray of hostages, the officers lack the angle for clear shots.

Gemento elbows a woman in the head, knocking her out of his way. He kicks a man in the back. Soon, he squeezes through the doorway. Some tear gas has drifted out here, but the smoke is lighter than in the ballroom. The hostages' expressions are less pained. Still unaware of the bombs' locations, they don't try to run outside, instead spread through the wing.

"Let's lock ourselves in the rooms," a woman yells.

Gemento follows a pack of people south, without a particular destination, just trying to get distance from the cops. In the crowd, he spots Ollie, jogging hand in hand with Rose. Pissed off because of the cops, pissed off because of Cole Maddox, pissed off because his son will never forgive him, Gemento needs a release.

"Hey Ollie," he says.

Ollie turns to him with a surprised expression.

Gemento shoots him. The bullet tears through Ollie's left cheek, and his hand splits from Rose's. His back slams into the wall as she and others scream. He falls to the floor, lifeless.

Gemento throws his original human shield down and grabs Rose.

46

The door of a room in the north wing swings open. The hostage who opened it darts inside. Others in the cramped hallway pile in behind him. As Gemento tugs Rose down the hallway, frightened party guests and hotel employees stagger out of his way, avoiding eye contact.

His outfit, announcing him as a Children of the Sun member, strikes fear in them, a benefit, but it can also identify him as a target to the cops. If he is going to get off this property alive, he can't do it looking like one of the most wanted men in Montana.

He eyes the crowd ahead, spotting a guy in a tuxedo who's a tad shorter than him, and a tad heavier, but close enough in size for his plan to work. Yanking Rose's forearm, Gemento picks up his pace, weaving through the throng, knocking people out the way, until right behind the man.

Gemento trails him toward a women's bathroom in the hall. Once the man is beside the door, Gemento clasps his neck and shoves him through it. The lady with him, wearing a wedding band, gasps.

Gemento points his pistol between her eyes and says, "Keep

moving, into the next open room. If I catch you out here, I'm going to shoot you, then your husband."

She lifts her hands in surrender. Her makeup is a mess from the tear gas, squiggles of eyeshadow extending to her temples. She scampers away.

Gemento enters the bathroom, pushing in Rose. The male hostage, with a mix of anger and confusion on his face, tries running out, then stops when noticing the pointed gun. Like his wife, he raises his hands.

"I don't want a problem," the guy says.

"Good," Gemento replies. "Then take off your clothes."

"What?"

"Take them off, or I kill your wife. I'll be sure to take my time with her."

"Uh, okay. Christ." The guy removes his tux jacket and begins unbuttoning his shirt.

"Faster."

He speeds up. Rose watches on, but her mind seems elsewhere. Tears trickle down her face, fresh ones, not from the gas. She must be upset Ollie is dead.

Within half a minute, the male hostage stands in just his socks and pinstriped boxers. He has an old scar over his abdomen that seems surgical.

"Get in a stall, on your knees," Gemento says.

The guy's eyes move to the closed bathroom door, as if considering the safety of his wife on the other side. He takes a deep breath, then drops to his knees in the nearest toilet stall.

"Hands together, on the toilet seat," Gemento says. "Eyes ahead, not at me." The man does as told. Gemento zip-ties his wrists around the toilet seat, then says to Rose, "You too, turn around, eyes away from me."

When she does as instructed, he removes his own clothes, bulletproof vest, and both his masks. Now is the first time all night that his face is exposed. He digs his hand into Rose's purse, pulls out her phone, and dumps it in the toilet. He doesn't want her snapping any pictures. Though the masks made him appear criminal, not wearing any opens him up to other risks.

Ahead of tonight's mission, he underwent facial-reconstructive surgery, as did the other Children of the Sun who came here. Even if the cops deduced Gemento's real identity, which was probable, any photos of William Laud in a government database would not match his current likeness, with its thinned nose and broadened jaw, not to mention alterations from black hair dye and green contacts.

What his current likeness does match is the photo on his fake passport, which he'll use to travel to Moldova under a phony name. However, between now and the flight, if the cops somehow obtain a clear image of his current-day face, it'll be sent to every airline in the US, making boarding a plane much more challenging.

Gemento puts on the man's clothes. The tux is a bit loose and the shoes a bit tight, but doable. He sticks his gun in the waist of the pants, then collects his phone, walkie-talkie, and some zip-ties from his original pants.

Over the radio, he reaches out to his remaining men. He feels bad so many of them have died, however, not close to as bad as when he lost Ella. Though he calls these guys his brothers, they're nothing like the family he once had. Still, he does have a bond with them. And they must work together, now more than ever. The more of them that remain alive and unarrested, the more support he'll have trying to leave the resort. He informs them to strip down and steal tuxedos so they can pass for hostages, like him.

In his pants pocket, Gemento finds the male hostage's wallet. Inside is an Alpine Grand keycard. "Tell me your room number,"

Gemento says. "If you give me the wrong one, you're going to be sorry."

"What...uh...what do you want to do in our room?"

Gemento kicks him in the abdomen, over his scar. The patent-leather shoe makes a splat sound against the bare flesh, which echoes through the bathroom.

"Your room number, not questions," Gemento says.

The man growls in pain. "Two thirty-two."

Gemento tosses the guy's phone in the toilet with Rose's, then says in her ear, "You're coming with me. In the hallway, if you open your mouth to anyone about who I am, or open your eyes and look at my face, you're going to be even sorrier than him."

He wraps his arm around her waist, as a husband would do to a wife, to not provoke any suspicion on hallway security cameras. Her perfume is a bit like the kind Ella would wear on special occasions. He angles his head down, preventing a clear view of his face on surveillance, and tells her to do the same.

They leave the bathroom. Even if she were stupid enough to talk, she'd have nobody to talk to. The corridor is empty. Most hostages must be locked down in rooms by now. He leads her into the stairwell, up to the second floor, and into empty room 232, in the east wing.

He'll stay here until the other men confirm they've found disguises. Then, before the helicopter brings over more cops, they'll attempt to escape the property.

47

Cole still kneels behind the lawn boulder. His injured eye continues to water. Through his impaired vision, he saw Rowack and his team hop off the SWAT chopper and sweep into the building. However, that was several minutes ago, and still no update from Shauna declaring victory. He calls her.

"Hey," she says. She sounds a bit out of breath, as if just talking at length. Voices chatter in the background.

"Did they get Gemento?"

"SWAT put down one terrorist in the ballroom and arrested a wounded one in the kitchen. Neither was Gemento, unfortunately."

"Where is he now?"

"They, um, they don't seem to know."

"They lost him?"

"First, the good news. Your buddy Eagle apparently started some sort of an uprising. The hostages stormed out of the ballroom and locked themselves in guest rooms."

Cole grins. Good stuff, Eagle.

"The bad news," Shauna says. "Gemento and the three terrorists still standing slipped away in the crowd. SWAT is searching every corner of the hotel. But it's a big place."

"Is that all the bad news?"

"No. Another hostage was shot in the hallway. We're still waiting on an ID."

Cole's grin fades. Another hostage joins the list with Melinda Raymon, Curtis Fitts, and Scott Zaddel. Cole imagines the pain their families are going through tonight. Spouses, siblings, parents, children, devastated. Those families deserve justice.

Even if the confiscated-crypto strategy worked, and the terrorists released the hostages, the police and FBI weren't going to pay them a million bucks and let them off. That was a ruse. The authorities were going to hunt for them on the outside. However, finding them among the general public would've been difficult. Capturing them while still in the hotel is a much better option.

"Gemento must have some plan for them to leave the Alpine Grand," Cole says. "It's probably already in motion. If SWAT doesn't arrest them soon, they can get away with this."

"Worst case, they do somehow sneak away. Yes, they avoid prison, at least unless we get lucky and find them. But the drone still maps out all the bombs and the cops still walk everybody out of the hotel by morning. With the Children of the Sun gone, no more hostages get killed. I'd call that a big success."

If the terrorists happen to come outside and veer Cole's way, of course he'd pick them off with his rifle. However, after the RPG operator went silent, he doubts they'd venture this direction, even if it were in their original exit plan.

A part of Cole wants to go inside and help SWAT bring these guys to justice. But he takes a deep breath and remains in place. His hurt eye would be a drawback in a life-or-death confrontation. Him leaving the safety of his current position wouldn't be fair to his daughter.

48

Children of the Sun member Lloyd Stratech is parked with his headlights off behind some tall evergreens in Timber Ridge, a couple hundred feet down the street from where the dickhead at the hotel, Cole Maddox, is said to live.

Thirty-three-year-old Lloyd has a mullet, a wispy reddish-blond moustache, and cheeks cratered from teenage acne. His old, dented pickup truck's original license plates were removed, replaced with ones screwed off a vehicle parked in the driveway of a random home in town. In the back seat is a yearbook stolen from the high school.

When Gemento first formed the Children of the Sun website and social-media pages, hundreds of thousands of people used them to vent online about their troubles, and found support from others in similar entanglements. However, that changed eleven months ago, when Gemento's wife died and he decided to branch the group out into the physical world, offer membership to a select few men, and carry out a mission with them. Though Lloyd is honored to be one of these men, he was hesitant to go into the hotel tonight, in case things turned bloody.

He's had an aversion to blood since childhood, when his dad used to strike his bare back with a mop handle until breaking skin.

Next to Lloyd in the passenger seat is another official group member, Dale. He's shorter and beefier than Lloyd, with a black goatee. Unlike Lloyd, Dale finished high school. A while ago, he used to work in an office, one of just a handful of Children of the Sun who ever had a desk job. But his company purchased a computer program that could do his job better, so they let him go.

Gemento instructed them to wear all white, so they could blend in with the snow when they snuck up to Maddox's house. With stores closed at this hour, they relied on spray-paint to get various clothing items from their mobile homes the right color. The outfits look a bit streaky, but okay.

"Shit," Lloyd says, peering between tree branches at Maddox's cabin through binoculars. "The cop car is still there."

The skin under Dale's lips puffs from chewing tobacco. He spits into an empty root beer can. "Then we still wait here."

"It's getting late, man. We were supposed to do it by now."

"We go up there with those pigs, not only aren't we getting back the crypto, we gonna get locked up. Only a matter of time before the police lump us in with the business at the hotel. We gonna get charged as terrorists, even though we didn't even set foot in that place. You know the prison time y'all get for terrorism?" He spits into the soda can. "Shit."

By now, Lloyd figured he'd own a house and make a decent enough living to get the attention of a decent enough woman. He maybe even would've had a kid or two. But after his factory job was given to some foreigner on the other side of the globe, he couldn't find another.

Years ago, when American companies made things here like they should, a street-smart guy like Lloyd would've had no hitches at all. He'd be a floor manager somewhere with an entire crew under him. But in the modern-day USA, no CEO is interested in a talented young man like him. They'd rather pay sub-minimum wage for sub-quality work overseas. The politicians who lie to get Lloyd's vote pretend they understand his issues, but they aren't looking out for him, either.

To make things worse, most of the country believes he has some sort of privilege just because he's White. If he's owed something good in America because of his skin color, nobody's ever told him where to claim it.

The future for a man like him looks even bleaker as all this tech mumbo-jumbo continues to infest the economy. Moldova would be different. He wouldn't need much to get some respect there. He could find a nice girl who appreciates him.

American women are just gold diggers, he's concluded. They don't recognize the value of a genuine man with a good heart. Rose Stallos is a perfect example, flaunting her ass on magazine pages and marrying some greedy billionaire. Though Lloyd despises the woman, he did stumble upon some old bathing-suit modeling photos of her on the internet and has jacked off to them at least seven times.

He opens the glovebox and grabs Dale's revolver.

"Whoa, whoa," Dale says.

"Those cops ain't going anywhere unless our boys at the hotel surrender, which we know they isn't. If we're gonna do this, we gotta tonight, while it's still dark."

Dale grunts.

"I'm getting us back our money," Lloyd says. "And we're buying that piece of land in Moldova."

"Rolling up on a cop with a gun is gonna get you even more prison—"

"Prison can't be much worse than the shit hole I live in now."

Dale gazes at him for a moment, then looks ahead, out into the storm. "I'm not going up there right now. But I'll swear to you, if you can take care of the cops, I'll help you drag the pregnant chick out of the cabin and we'll haul ass out of here."

This son of a bitch wants to take no risk, yet enjoy the upside. Though Lloyd is angry, arguing will only eat up more time. He takes a deep breath and reaches into the back seat, grabbing two white towels with eye holes cut out and a roll of duct tape. The men take turns taping a towel mask over each other's head.

Lloyd steps out into the cold. The revolver is heavier than he imagined. The weight makes the reality of all this set in. His heart booms. Since the police car is facing the road, he doesn't head toward Maddox's driveway, but jogs onto a neighbor's property on the same side of the street. He skulks across the snowy lawn into the backyard, then into the strip of woods that extends behind multiple homes.

Hunching over, Lloyd catches his breath for a bit, then paces through the brush to the rear of Maddox's land. Through the binoculars, Lloyd spots two heads in the cop car, the backs to him.

He's never shot anybody. He's never even punched anybody. When he was picked on in school, he thought about fighting back a few times, but never did. Maybe his dad is to blame. Just before Lloyd got beaten, his father would whisper in his ear, "Try to resist, and next you're getting the mop up your little asshole."

In a crouch, Lloyd moves through the backyard toward the police car, approaching from an angle, trying to staying out of the rearview mirror. The snow soaks his shoes and the bottoms of his sweats.

He gets closer to the two cops, his heart rate climbing. Even closer. The guy in the driver's seat looks young, still in his twenties. He has a tight crew cut that seems no more than a couple days old. For all Lloyd knows, he could be a great dude. For a second, Lloyd considers turning around and calling this off. But then he's reminded of what his leader Gemento says about police, how they contribute to keeping men like Lloyd down.

A bullet from the revolver smashes through the police car's rear glass and goes into the head of the young cop. Blood spatters the front windshield.

As Lloyd aims at the second cop, the man ducks. His car door opens. Panicking, Lloyd thinks to take cover behind the driver's side. However, before he can, a bullet penetrates his stomach. The force knocks him to the ground.

His adrenaline is so high, he doesn't feel the pain. The cop emerges from around the bumper to fire again, but Lloyd gets a shot off first. The round catches the cop in the chest. He topples, drops his gun, and clutches his wound with both hands.

With a shaky grip, Lloyd aims his weapon in case the policeman gets up and makes another move. But he doesn't. Within half a minute, his spasming stops. He's dead.

Lloyd lets out a breath of relief. But it hurts. The adrenaline spike must've subsided a bit, though his heart still pounds. He glances at his stomach. Blood spurts out of it.

His feet go numb. He tells himself the numbness is just from the snow, though he knows this isn't true. He gropes for his phone in his pocket and calls Dale.

"You did it?" Dale asks, a note of optimism in his voice.

"The cops. But you need to..." His voice becomes faint. He musters up energy and forces out, "Get her and help me." His hand isn't strong enough to hold onto the phone. It falls onto the snow.

A second-story light goes on in the cabin. The gunshots must've woken up the pregnant woman. Dale speeds up the driveway, jumps out of the truck, and surveys the bloody mess around the police car. His towel mask is a tad lopsided.

"Jesus Christ," he mutters.

Lloyd lacks the vigor to talk, but can point at the lit window. Dale needs to snatch the woman before more police arrive. He seems to get the message, picking up the revolver. He shoots a first-level window, reaches through to unlock it, and crawls inside.

The woman yells, "Declan, lock your door and stay in your room."

Within a minute, another gunshot comes from the house. In the lit window, behind the sheer curtain, appears the silhouette of a male body. Dale must've shot his way into her room through the doorknob. The woman screams. But the sound is soft in Lloyd's ears. His legs and half his torso are numb.

Within another minute, the front door flies open. Dale emerges with a gorgeous young lady. She looks like the sort of woman Lloyd pictured himself ending up with when he was young, before he knew the harsh realities of the world. She becomes dark and fuzzy in his vision, along with everything else.

"Get up, let's go," Dale says to him.

The rest of Lloyd's body goes numb.

49

The blood from the corpses swells across the snow toward Lacey's bare feet. She wears just little shorts and a tee shirt, a slight curve to it from her and Cole's baby. With his boot, the man clenching her forearm pushes on the leg of the other guy in a towel mask and says, "Lloyd?" The one on the ground doesn't move. "Fuck."

Lacey's hazy mind considers if this is a nightmare. Her last memory is going to bed. But the windy tap of snowflakes on her arms and legs feels real. A robbery, maybe. But the masked man doesn't ask for anything or go back into the house to take anything.

"Help," she screams, toward the two cops.

As she feared, they're more than injured, no reaction.

She punches the masked man's gloved hand, but his grip doesn't break. It tightens. He pulls her to a pickup truck and shoves her onto the passenger seat. She crosses her arms over her stomach to protect the baby. Her elbow whacks the center console.

The man leans over her. He smells like paint. Through the frayed holes in his mask, one oval-shaped, the other a circle, are eyes that seem ashamed to look into hers. He reaches under her and tears something off her seat, scraping against the bottom of her thigh. A roll of duct tape. He pries her hands away from the baby and tapes them together. She knees him in the rib, but he's unaffected. She attempts to kick him, but he clasps her ankle and yanks it down to her other. He wraps them in tape and slams the door closed.

The pulses on the undersides of her bound wrists drum against each other. As the man circles the pickup toward the driver's side, she debates trying to hop away. But no. Not only would he catch up to her, if she slipped, her stomach would bash into the ground. She sits still, overwhelmed with helplessness, as he gets behind the wheel.

"What do you want from me?" she asks.

He says nothing. He hits the gas pedal and the truck coasts down the driveway onto the road. Whatever this is, more cops might come and rescue her. Her son must've called 9-1-1 by now. Though he wouldn't have seen the truck's license plate, or even the make and model, the police could set up checkpoints, looking for her in any car that attempts to leave the area.

He turns onto a windy road penned in by massive evergreens. His breath is heavy, his mask moving by his mouth. At a stoplight, instead of turning right toward the highway, he makes a left to go higher up the mountain.

She didn't expect this. With a kidnap, she'd assume he'd want to reach the highway ASAP, before any checkpoints were set up, and get far from Timber Ridge. If he's staying in town for now, when he does leave, he must plan to without her. That makes for two options. Before he goes, he lets her out of the car alive, or dead.

Her throat constricts. She doesn't quite feel like she's suffocating, but just one notch down. The road slopes even higher. No tire marks on the snow ahead. No other vehicles must've been up here for a while.

Recalling what the doctor said about stress hormones and pregnancy, she closes her eyes and tries to calm herself. In her psychology classes, she's learned the physical power of thought. Though she isn't safe, she tries to trick herself into believing she is.

She closes her eyes and pictures Cole, the most protective person she's ever known. If he weren't at that hotel for the night, when this masked man broke into the house, she would've liked to have seen what happened to him. She imagines Cole is with her now, in the backseat, his arms around her, one hand on her stomach, just the way he keeps it when they're lying in bed. This works. Her heart rate eases a bit.

The truck climbs the mountain in silence besides the soft screech of the windshield wipers. In about fifteen minutes, it stops. When she opens her eyes, she sees they're in a small clearing of a forest. The snowflakes seem thicker up here, like marbles, and the sky even blacker.

"Stay still," the man says. "I'm gonna take your picture."

"Why?"

No answer. He fishes his phone out of his pocket and taps a few buttons. He pulls the revolver from the waist of his pants and moves it toward her baby bump.

"No," she screams, spinning her back to him. The pickup's worn leather seat scratches against her cheek.

"Let's not make this hard," he says. "Turn over."

She doesn't, hunched over in the fetal position, trembling.

"For now, it's just a picture," he says. "I'm not gonna shoot your baby unless our demands are ignored." He jerks her shoulder, flipping her back over. "But I will be forced to start hurting you if you don't let me take the picture. I'm a nice guy, believe me. I'm just doing what I gotta. It'll make me upset, but if you don't stay still, I'm gonna have to start smashing your cute little toes with the butt of my gun."

She gazes out at the deep wilderness. Nobody is coming up here to help her. Her best bet is to just do as this man says.

She again closes her eyes, unable to bring herself to see a gun so close to her daughter. She's reminded of the doctor's office as a little girl, waiting on the table with her eyelids together, anticipating the tip of a needle. When she feels the metal tip of the revolver, she winces.

"That's it," he says. "Nice and still. Let me get that pretty face in the shot." In a moment, the gun goes away. "You did good."

When she opens her eyes, she catches him staring at the outline of her bra-less breasts. He looks away, fidgeting. Despite having all the physical power over her, he radiates a pathological insecurity. He seems like a weak man who's had a difficult life. But she isn't comforted by this. Men without much to lose are some of the most dangerous.

"I just want this to be over," she says. "Those demands of me you mentioned, what are they? I'll do whatever you need."

"There's nothing you can do. Your boyfriend is the one who needs to do something. You wait here with me and hope he does."

Her mind struggles to find a connection to Cole. But one wouldn't surprise her. As protective as he is of her, he is also protective of other people. Twice before, his efforts to help somebody else caused a backlash that affected her. But this time is different. It's much worse.

At this stage of the pregnancy, the doctor says their daughter is only about the size of a sweet potato. Tonight, Cole put her at risk, too. Though Lacey fights the thought, she can't help but envision what a bullet would do to someone that tiny.

50

Gemento's piss splashes in the toilet of room 232 of the Alpine Grand. He's had to go for hours, but didn't want to risk leaving the safety of the ballroom for a leak break, or wet his pants, like many of the hostages did, and undermine his air of authority. 232's bathroom light is on, the rest off. He stares at the triangle of bottles by the tub. The conditioner is named M. Laureux Formula No. 4 Bamboo Nourisher. Fucking rich people.

He flushes, washes his hands, and leans against the doorframe with his arms crossed, facing Rose, who sits on the bed, blindfolded by a pillowcase. A soft glow spills onto her. She's still crying, tears squeezing out beneath the blindfold. However, she seems to be trying to resist them, her top teeth biting her lower lip.

Large energy companies tend to be run by men with hardened dispositions and decades of experience analyzing numbers on spreadsheets. Her board must've been wary to give control to a woman who broke into the industry because of who she was fucking, then worked in a non-quantitative department like PR. To lessen their concerns, he supposes she developed habits to hide traces of her personality that could be associated with softness, including the show of emotion.

His phone vibrates. He opens a photo message from Dale, a man sent to Timber Ridge. In it is a petrified-looking pregnant woman with a gun pointed at her stomach. A flurry of excitement builds in Gemento's chest. Not only does he still have a chance to get off the property without arrest, he has a chance to get back the $2.725 million.

He sends the picture to Hectus, with the text:

Good news. What's your status?

Gemento then sends the photo to the policewoman, along with a message for her to pass to Cole Maddox.

"Why'd you have to kill him?" Rose asks. She must be referring to Ollie.

"He tried to convince me you did nothing wrong."

"He was a good man."

"He loved you, didn't he?"

Her dress sparkles in the dim light from the bathroom. She's still for a moment, then nods *yes*.

"Did you love him?" he asks.

She's still for a moment, then shakes her head *no*. "But I cared for him. Like a brother, I guess. Do you have a brother?"

"No."

"If you did, I'm sure you wouldn't want to watch him get shot in the head."

"Probably not."

"Are you going to kill me?"

"I thought about it. But no...I'm not going to kill you."

Though her posture is still tight, some of the tension in her shoulders releases. "Why not?"

"I'm going to be leaving soon. As much as I'd like you to admit what you did on camera, without any hostage at gunpoint, I know you'll stall. And I don't have time for that, now. If I kill you, you won't be able to tell America the truth. But if I let you live, I hope you'll decide to come clean on your own, one day. All the people who died tonight, Ollie and everyone else, died because of what you did to me. If you cared about them, don't let those losses be in vain. You and Hampton should confess. It'll lighten your conscience."

"I did something a little iffy to get a construction project approved. You murdered multiple human beings. And now you're lecturing me about my conscience?"

"In war, when an American kills an enemy, we call it patriotism. This, what happened tonight at the hotel, this was my war. It didn't have the approval of Congress, like the sorts of wars your billionaire friends start, but it's no different."

She taps a finger on her thigh a few times. It makes a light crackling sound on the dress material. "I'm sorry about what happened to your wife. I found a news article on my phone about it."

He gives her a reflexive nod of gratitude, forgetting for a moment she can't see him.

"If whatever we did somehow led to that," she says, "I hope you realize that was never my intention. That would've been impossible to predict." She takes a big breath, her chest rising, then exhales. "I just...I was under a lot of pressure for fast results with the stock price. What the company put me through...it wasn't fair."

"Through my whole life, people would say the world isn't fair. I never quite believed them. But now, I think they were right."

The room is quiet for a while.

"I could go for a fucking drink," she says.

He realizes he could too, so walks to the minibar and grabs a small bottle of Jack Daniel's for himself. For some reason, he decides to grant her wish, and gets her a drink, too, a tiny Absolut vodka.

"Thanks," she says, her hand finding the bottle he presses

against her thigh. She sounds somewhat surprised he extended her this little pleasure.

They unscrew the tops and swig. Her sip continues after his. She finishes her bottle in one gulp and drops it on the bed beside the pillow stripped of its case.

His phone vibrates. A text from Hectus:

We found tuxedos. A man on the outside is getting into place. Once he confirms a safe lat-long, we're all getting out of here. Should be just a few more minutes.

Gemento downs the rest of his Jack Daniel's in celebration.

51

Cole watches the hotel's front from behind the lawn boulder, the clarity in his untreated right eye down to about fifty percent, the edges of all objects hazy. Even so, he's been able to see that no terrorists have emerged from the building. SWAT could've found them by now.

He receives a text message. When he notices Shauna's name, he expects she's going to inform him that Gemento and the others have been arrested. However, she relays something quite different:

I'm sorry for doing this, but I was instructed to show you something. And to tell you that you have until sunrise to give back the money.

He stares at the screen. In a moment, a photo shows up. Of Lacey. His breathing speeds up. The cloud of steam rising from his mouth grows.

His thoughts rush around his head as he tries to make sense of what he's looking at. The terrorists must've somehow gotten around the Timber Ridge cops. And beforehand, they must've gotten his address. They could have a member with access to a DMV database. But the anti-government Children of the Sun don't seem like the type to hold government jobs. The more probable explanation is that someone here betrayed him. Only one hostage would know his address by memory, Ollie.

The barrel of a revolver is up to Lacey's stomach like the ultrasound wand at last week's doctor's appointment. Cole couldn't just stand back when the terrorists infiltrated the hotel. Unlike the Stallos employees, he had to do something. And this is where that decision led.

His head spinning, he places a hand on the ground to prevent himself from tipping over, out of his cramped track in the snow and onto a bomb. If he were like the Stallos employees, his fiancee would be sound asleep. His sweet-potato-sized daughter wouldn't have a deadly weapon pointed at her. And when she was born, she could go to any school she wanted to, because her daddy would have a high-paying job and he'd be able to take care of it.

He is still for a while, the snow falling on him as he thinks about all that could've been and all that may never be. The cold, wet fabric of his sweatshirt and jeans cling to his skin. He takes a deep breath and texts Shauna, asking for Gemento's number, then calls it.

"Who is this?" Gemento asks.

"It's me."

Gemento is silent for a moment. "I had a feeling that picture would get your attention."

The easy answer to this problem is to just give Gemento back the money. However, in a strange way, the money is the only thing keeping Lacey and the baby alive. Cole killed many terrorists tonight. The remaining ones would want retribution. The way to make him suffer most is to shoot Lacey in the stomach, which they may do the moment after he gives back the crypto and loses all his leverage.

"You have a son, right?" Cole asks.

"Yes. But I don't think he ever wants to see me again. If you are going to try to appeal to me as a family man and attempt to change my mind, it's not going to work. I don't have a family anymore. The only thing I have left is a chance at a new beginning. And I need that money for that. Hopefully you make the right decision by sunrise, or you'll have nothing left but a chance at a new beginning, too." Gemento hangs up.

52

Cole gazes at the face of the dead RPG operator. His sunglasses are on a slant, his mouth open a tad. One of his teeth is chipped, not from their fight tonight, but some event in his past. The wind has taken on a lower pitch. Instead of a whistle in the sky, it sounds like static on an old TV. Cole shivers.

His phone vibrates. It snaps him out of an introspective daze. He answers Shauna's call. "Yeah?" he says. His voice sounds different in his ear. It's quieter, a flatness to it.

"Any progress from your call with Gemento?"

"No." He closes his eyes. "I think I made a mistake. Maybe the worst mistake of my life."

"This isn't your fault."

"It is."

"You were just trying to protect the people in the hotel. If it weren't for you, we never would've gotten a SWAT team in there this quickly. You couldn't have foreseen...that photo...when you first stepped in to help the hostages. You can't see into the future. Don't blame yourself for this."

"No, I can't see into the future, but I've always tried to shape it, at least as much as I could. That's why a soldier goes to war, for a good future for the people in the country."

"And you did secure a good future for us. That's why millions of people from all over the world still want to move to America. And almost all the hundreds of millions already here, stay."

"If I made anything better for all of them, great. But I apparently can't even look out for my own child's future, and she isn't even born yet."

"That's not how to view it."

"All the Stallos guys played it safe tonight, just tried to stay alive and get back home. Their kids are sleeping in peace right now, while mine has a revolver pointed at her through my fiancee's stomach. Who's the better dad?"

"The reason men like that can play it safe is because they know men like you are out there."

Cole looks down. The wind, which has grown heavier, ruffles his sweatshirt.

"I'm a parent," Shauna says. "Hopefully, by now, I've learned a thing or two about what makes a good one. You know what the main thing is, the one that matters most? Being able to take an unexpected dilemma and handle it on the fly. The stuff you plan for, that's easy. That always works out somehow. When that baby is born and starts growing up, situations are going to come at you that you never could've imagined. Having the instincts to deal with them is what makes the difference."

He inhales cold air through his nose and lets out an audible exhale.

"This thing with your fiancee and daughter," Shauna says, "I'm not going to sugarcoat it. It's horrible. That's a nasty photo you just had to process. But you've been taking on nasty stuff all night and coming out on top. This is just another unexpected dilemma. So get your head out of your ass, start acting like Cole Maddox, and handle it."

He takes a couple more deep, cold breaths. "I'll try my best."

"The four remaining Children of the Sun are still out there, so be careful."

"I have to go."

"If there was something I could do to help, I would."

"I know."

"All right. Bye Cole." She ends the call.

He bends his body into the arch position it was in earlier and labors through the snow to the duffel bag that's been on the ground. His shot arm trembles. He returns to the boulder, sticks various pieces of gear into the bag, and straps it to his back.

As he and Diaz went over earlier, the Children of the Sun didn't pull up to the hotel in vehicles. Instead, they must've been dropped off on a street bordering the woods. The police already have roadblocks set up on any street within reasonable walking distance through the brush. The terrorists, smart enough to assume that, shouldn't be leaving here on foot. They'd want to travel deep into the wilderness, then come out on a rural road miles from here, where an ally would be waiting to pick them up.

Though the Alpine Grand's parking lot is packed with dozens of high-performance cars, they couldn't pass through the forest's tight-together trees. However, another type of vehicle on the property could.

The snowmobiles.

Cole spotted them earlier, under a hut, far on the west side of the property. From the northeast, he could reach them much faster if he went back inside the hotel and jogged to the end of the west wing. However, he'd be exposed to a four-on-one terrorist ambush in close quarters. Instead, he takes the longer outdoor route, moving in the arduous arch with his rifle on the ground to check for bombs.

Despite the freezing temperature, his lungs are hot. The snow makes a loud chewing noise as he pushes through it.

When he veers onto the northwest portion of the lawn, something at the edge of the surrounding woods catches his attention. He stops and kneels in the track he's made in the snow. With the binoculars, he takes a closer look. A pair of hands are bound to the bark of a tree. Forearms rise from the deep snow, yet the rest of the body is invisible beneath it. The hands are motionless. Diaz mentioned a third security guard, still unaccounted for. That must be him. Frozen to death.

A thought pierces Cole's mind of Lacey ending up the same way by sunrise, dead in the woods, their baby dead inside her.

53

Gemento steps out of room 232, his head angled down for any security cameras. Rose is zip-tied to the bed, the landline phone unplugged. Though the cops will find her during a room-by-room search, since she didn't get a look at his current face, she won't have much to tell them.

Moments ago, a Children of the Sun member on the outside informed Gemento that he's found a safe spot, on an unmonitored road that borders the wilderness, twenty-one miles from the Alpine Grand. It leads to a highway. And in the van are a change of clothes for the four men here. If they can reach the rendezvous latitude-longitude on snowmobiles, getting to the airport for their morning flights will be easy.

Gemento paces down the hallway. *Thunt, thunt, thunt.* That damn noise again. Out the window, the SWAT helicopter has returned, hovering over the ballroom. A second team of cops will swing inside any second.

His heart rate accelerating, Gemento takes the stairwell to the first floor and peeks into an east-wing corridor. It's empty, at least for now. Desperate to get behind a locked door, the hostages jammed themselves into rooms by the ballroom. The first team of

SWAT cops must be around there, questioning them about what Gemento looks like, questions that won't receive satisfying answers. But now that backup has arrived, the police search should widen through the halls, which will be an issue.

Gemento walks toward the four-way intersection. Though running would get him there faster, if a cop happened to notice, Gemento would look suspicious. He tries to come off as a hostage, opening his mouth a tad, slumping his shoulders, as if exhausted and overwhelmed. He passes remnants of the stampede, a high heel, a busted pair of eyeglasses, a broken phone, a couple trampled-flat purses.

Around the bend, he notices a man's arm, cloaked in black. In a few more paces, Gemento makes out a tuxedo, then two more. His three guys, with their faces turned away from ceiling surveillance cameras, are in position.

Gemento looks in all directions to verify nobody is watching. "Good to go?"

Hectus gives him a thumbs-up while the other two nod. They advance to the intersection and head west. During reconnaissance of the Alpine Grand, a couple Children of the Sun stayed here as guests. They went on the snowmobile tour and made a mental note of where the guide kept the keys, in a small wooden cabinet under the parking hut. That hut, off the end of the west wing, can be accessed via the door in the spa that leads to the Jacuzzis.

The four men walk that direction at a brisk pace, Gemento leading. On the rug around the spa entrance, a few shards of broken glass glint. Nearby are spots of dry blood. All this must be a byproduct of Cole Maddox's attack. Through the cracked door pane is movement. Someone is in the spa.

Gemento freezes. The other three Children of the Sun seem to sense something is wrong, stopping too.

"Who's there?" a deep male voice asks from inside, in an authoritative tone. He doesn't sound like a hostage.

Gemento's heart beats even faster. He takes a moment to gather his thoughts. "Our rooms are on the third floor," he says, putting an artificial note of confusion in his voice to sound like a hostage. "We don't know if it's safe to go up there. Are you a police officer? Can you help us?"

The SWAT cop opens the door, glass slivers clinking underneath it. His gas mask up on his head, his chestnut-brown hair curling around it, he looks like the gym teacher Gemento had in sixth grade. The spa's floor is soaked. Lying on the wet marble is the lifeless body of one of Gemento's men. Though Gemento tries to conceal his anger, his expression must indicate it, because the cop's eyes squint with skepticism. His fingers wrap the handle of his holstered gun.

"Move away," the cop says. "All of you. Backs against the wall."

"Did we do something wrong?" Gemento asks.

"Backs against the wall."

"We just want to—"

The cop draws his gun and points it at Gemento's face. "Now."

"Okay, Officer." Gemento raises his hands. His three men do, too, and they all backpedal to the hallway wall.

If the cop radios backup over here, escaping on the snowmobiles will become next to impossible. Even if he doesn't call backup, and the Children of the Sun were fortunate enough to somehow get outside, this policeman has seen all their faces, not to mention, can approximate their heights and weights. Airlines would be looking out for men with their descriptions. Gemento could try to shoot this guy. But a gunshot would draw even more cops than the radio.

"I'm going to need IDs on all of you," the policeman says. "Do not reach for your wallets. Turn around, put your palms on the wall, and I'll collect your wallets from your pockets."

"Do as he says," Hectus replies. As the Children of the Sun face the wall, Hectus gives Gemento a quick look in the eye.

The cop frisks the man to Hectus's side and asks, "What pocket is your wallet in?"

"It's up in my room."

The officer, who keeps patting him down, doesn't find a wallet, but does seem to notice something protruding from the man's rear waist. The cop's brow creases. He reaches under the tux jacket and yanks out a pistol.

As he goes for his shoulder radio, Hectus's right hand separates from the wall and dips into a pocket. He does a 180 and digs his switchblade into the side of the officer's neck.

Blood squirts out, a unified, thick stream, like that from a water fountain. The cop's jaw hangs. His tongue spasms. Hectus's hand remains on the knife even as the cop totters backward. Hectus drags the blade to the side, shredding the man's throat. His lifeless body drops to the floor with a clunk, blood still pumping out of it.

Hectus waves the Children of the Sun into the spa. The air in here smells like flowers. They traverse the wet floor, slipping a bit, but staying on their feet. They exit into the northwest courtyard. Splayed on the ground by the Jacuzzis are the headshot corpses of two more of their men, additional casualties of Cole Maddox.

These two were biological brothers, young men from Louisiana. They loved to joke around. Gemento first connected with them online after they wrote a series of posts about their mother's passing. She was diagnosed with a bad, yet curable, illness. The medical-insurance company misled the family about coverage.

Buried deep in the paperwork, in ambiguous language, were various ways for the firm to avoid paying for certain treatments. The boys burnt through the small inheritance their father left the family, in the hope of saving their mother, with nothing left over for a lawyer. Despite their efforts, the out-of-pocket care they could afford wasn't enough.

If Cole Maddox does as told and gives back the crypto, Gemento considered honoring his word and freeing his fiancee. But no. Maddox killed too many good men, good men who just wanted a fresh start. Though the thought of executing an innocent woman and the baby inside her is unpleasant, what Maddox did to the Children of the Sun was just as unpleasant.

Avoiding bombs, Gemento, Hectus, and the other two sprint across the lawn to the snowmobile hut. Vehicles marked 1 through 8 are parked in two rows. Gemento finds the wooden cabinet. It's locked. He shoots the keyhole. Slivers of wood fly all over as the door swings open. He grabs keys 3 and 5, paired to the snowmobiles at the head of each row.

He tosses a key to one of his men and climbs onto snowmobile 5. Hectus sits on the seat behind him, while the other two get on 3. The engines start, growling. The headlights cut through the night, snowflakes dancing in the glow. Snowmobile 3 pulls out first. It weaves around a couple of trees and a boulder toward the woods. Gemento follows.

Just before the vehicle ahead reaches the forest, a loud noise goes off, distinct from the engines. An object whizzes through the air. The front snowmobile lifts off the ground in a fiery explosion. Its men are catapulted off. One goes into a violent roll, screaming, slapping at the flames engulfing his body. The other lies face down, not reacting to the fire charring him. He's already dead.

Gemento realizes they were just hit with the RPG.

54

Cole hides behind a large evergreen with the RPG over his shoulder, smoke wafting from the end. On the other side of the cloud, the still-functional snowmobile zooms by him into the forest.

Based on body type, Gemento appears to be driving, with a brawny guy on back. Though Cole has two more rockets in the duffel bag, he can't fire them at the remaining vehicle. Gemento must be stopped from escaping, yet kept alive so he can call off the hit on Lacey.

Cole throws down the RPG, grabs his rifle, and presses it down on the snow. He goes down into the uncomfortable, bomb-avoidance arch and scrabbles across the ground. After ten feet or so, he reaches Gemento's tracks.

Cole sprints within them to the hut and jumps on a snowmobile. Stretching his arm to an open cabinet, he snatches the key for vehicle 2, then turns on the engine. He yanks the duffel bag from his back to his front, slips the rifle inside, and pulls the strap back.

His headlights illuminating Gemento's tracks, Cole zips onto them. He races between two evergreens, their branches slapping his shoulders. The path through the forest is narrow, rocky, and hilly. He can't see Gemento's snowmobile, yet can hear the thrum of the engine, quite a way ahead.

The tracks curve around a log. When Cole makes the sharp turn, snow kicks up the cuff of his jeans, chilling his ankle. The path straightens for about fifty feet, then veers around a dense cluster of trees. Needing to close the gap between him and the terrorists, Cole doesn't slow down on the turn. He jerks the handlebars left. His injured forearm strains to hold on. His pain deepens.

Ahead, something flickers in the darkness. Gemento's headlights. The snowmobile climbs a hill. It's visible for about two seconds before vanishing on the other side.

Snow smacks Cole's face. Gemento's headlights return. He scales an even bigger hill. He's visible for a few seconds longer than last time before again disappearing.

Gemento, who must be aware of his tail, seems to be taking the most dangerous route possible through the woods, as if trying to cause his pursuer to crash. An even bigger and steeper hill is ahead, followed by another, bigger and steeper yet.

The nose of Cole's snowmobile slants downward. The heavy vehicle rumbles down a slope. Cole is tossed around, but hangs onto the handlebars, clenching the seat with his thighs for extra support.

His engine hums as he hits a straightaway. He follows an S-shape around a series of tall aspen trees, his headlights bringing out the black-oval marks on their white barks. The ground angles upward. He gives the snowmobile more gas. The two skis up front slide around. One knocks into a rock, shaking him. But, clutching with his arms and legs, he keeps the vehicle steady.

Gemento's headlights are out of view. He must be on the backside of the second to last visible hill. Cole reaches a clearing and skids to a stop. He rips the duffel bag off his back, pulls out the rifle, and stands on his snowmobile. In a moment, Gemento's lights surface. He rises up the final hill. Unaware of what's on the other side, Cole should stop him now.

Peering through the rifle scope, Cole tries to focus on the terrorist leader, lit only by headlights, most of the woods masked in darkness, complicating the shot. The wind, the moving target, and Cole's bad eye make the shot even harder.

He adjusts his scope for distance and follows his opponents' snowmobile, estimating its speed as it moves along the crosshair reticles. When lining up a sniper shot prior to the SWAT helicopter's arrival, he approximated a wind velocity. Since the wind has strengthened, he modifies the figure for his current calculation.

Gemento ascends the hill, about halfway up. Cole focuses on his target's shoulder, wanting to strike him in a place that'll cause him to crash, not die.

Cole waits for Gemento to emerge on the other side of a grove of trees, then lets out the air in his lungs. He avoids another breath, as it'll cause his stilled body to move a touch, which could throw the bullet off the necessary trajectory. Though he wants to shoot the shoulder, he aims a bit ahead of it, accounting for the time the bullet must travel through the air at this distance, aligned with the velocity of the snowmobile and the wind.

The only part of his body that moves is his index finger. It presses the trigger. *Pachoom.*

Gemento's snowmobile stops. However, his hands remain on the handlebars, his shoulder unfazed. With his injured eye, Cole's aim was off. Gemento and the other terrorist glance upward. He must've missed high.

The snowmobile starts moving again. It climbs farther up the hill, again vanishing behind trees. Cole recalibrates the math in his head, factoring in a reducing value for height. When Gemento appears from behind the trees, the snowmobile is about three quarters up the slope. Cole aims.

Pachoom. Gemento's left arm splits from the handlebars. A hit.

His right hand remains on the vehicle, still working the throttle. On terrain that steep, if he let off the gas, the snowmobile could slide backward. Steering with just one hand, he swerves. His left hand returns to its grip and he tries to straighten the snowmobile, but at the high speed, can't. At the top of the hill, the nose bashes into a tree. He and the other terrorist fly off and tumble out of view. The vacant snowmobile rolls the same way.

Cole packs his rifle back up and drives through his opponents' tracks. He negotiates a large hill, then the even larger one, and stops on the small patch of flat land at the top. To keep the cops out of the woods, the Children of the Sun claim to have planted bombs deep in the forest, so Cole remains careful with the terrain. He jumps off his seat into the roll marks in the snow left by his enemies' vehicle.

He crouches behind his snowmobile for cover in case they somehow held onto their weapons. But no bullets come. He pulls off his bag, frees his rifle, and peeks around the vehicle, down the backside of the hill.

At the bottom, the terrorists' snowmobile is on its side. Its headlights shine across a glassy surface. Gazing through the rifle scope, Cole makes out a frozen pond. The vehicle's impact must've cracked the ice, a zigzagging fracture extending from it to the land.

On the frozen pond, Gemento lies on his stomach, in a puddle of blood from his shoulder wound, while the second guy is on a knee, wobbling as if dazed.

A thrill runs through Cole. He has a clear shot on the second guy. This should all be over soon. But the thrill dissipates when Cole notices Gemento isn't moving. The crash could've killed him. If so, Cole would want to capture the living terrorist to call off the threat to Lacey.

However, Cole doesn't know anything about this man. Even physical force may not sway him to do the right thing. Gemento, on the other hand, is a known entity. Cole is confident the guy has a heart, even if it's been buried under a lot of scar tissue. William Laud, the former family man, has the capacity somewhere in him to spare the life of an innocent pregnant woman. And he may still be alive, just unconscious. So Cole doesn't kill either opponent.

The second terrorist rises to his feet and pats his back, as if checking for a gun that's no longer there. Though Cole shouldn't end his life, he needs to slow him down, so blasts a round through his thigh.

The guy's right leg blows backward and he plummets face-first onto the ice. He seems tough, getting up right away. Leaking blood, he crawls behind his snowmobile for cover and gropes at something in the shadows.

A bang from a pistol fills the forest. A tree branch two feet to Cole's side explodes in slivers. He ducks his head behind his snowmobile. Another bang. His vehicle shakes. If the guy hit it from down there with just a pistol, he's a good shot. Even though he needs Cole alive to get back the crypto, fearing for his own life, the man could've made the decision to try to kill. If Cole dies, Lacey and the baby have a high chance of dying, too.

Cole sticks the barrel of his rifle on his seat, keeping his head low. He'd like to shoot this guy's other leg, but he's hidden behind his snowmobile. At the edge of Cole's scope, though, he notices that Gemento is alive, seeing slight movements from his hands and feet. The loud gunfire must've awakened him.

Another bullet zings Cole's way, destroying his windshield, fragments landing in the snow. Cole crouches back down. Now that Gemento is breathing, the second terrorist can die. Cole fires a no-look cover round his direction, then peeks over his seat. The man is still hidden, so Cole shoots the nearby crack in the pond surface. He blasts half a dozen bullets into it. The sheet of ice the terrorist is on begins to move.

"Shit," he shouts. "Get on land."

The guy clambers across the breaking surface. Semi-conscious Gemento, who's farther from solid ground, struggles to get footing on the ice. He attempts to crawl, but his shot arm gives out. The fracture in the surface widens. The front of the terrorists' snowmobile dips into the dark water. No longer using the sinking vehicle as cover, the second terrorist is exposed, just as Cole planned. Aiming at his head, Cole fires.

But the man seems to have anticipated the shot. He alters his course, moving on a slant. The bullet misses, striking a rock. He dives off the shaky ice onto the snowy ground and scrabbles behind a tree. Cole's jaw clenches.

Gemento is still flailing around on the chaotic ice. The dark, deadly water closes in on him.

Cole fires a round at the western larch tree the second terrorist is behind, then runs out from the safety of the snowmobile and descends the hill, staying within the roll marks. A bullet whizzes past his head, tearing through pine needles inches away. Cole finds cover behind another tree. He fires a shot his opponent's way, then runs farther down the hill, toward Gemento, whose lower body is now submerged in the frigid water.

A bang echoes. Cole's torso hitches to the side. A hot pain tears through him, a couple inches above his left hip, just beneath the bulletproof vest. He falls and rolls down the steep hill. The weight of his body drops onto his arm, squashing his wrist against the rifle. The gun slips out of his hand as he keeps tumbling down the path his opponents did.

He becomes dizzy. His hip whacks a big tree. It stops his fall, but packs yet another pain into him. He drags his bleeding body behind the bark for cover. He glances at his rifle, out of reach. His pistol, up in the duffel bag, is even farther away.

A wild slapping sound comes from the water. The pond surface has ruptured into various slabs. With one healthy arm and nothing to grab onto but unstable ice, Gemento could drown. The whole of the terrorists' snowmobile has been sucked into the water, its headlights gone. The only light in the woods is faint, from Cole's vehicle atop the hill.

He peeks around the tree in the direction of the shooter. In a few seconds, a new light pops on. The circular beam is wide, yet doesn't extend far. It seems to be coming from a cellphone flashlight.

Cole crawls farther down the hill, staying away from the light, staying hidden. He snaps a branch off a tree, the sound concealed by Gemento treading water. Cole leaves the safe path of the roll marks, using the branch to check for bombs. Gemento, fighting for his life, doesn't notice him in the darkness. Cole moves through the dense snow to the rim of the pond.

The second terrorist fires a round toward the roll marks. His light beam rushes that direction, as if he's running, then stops.

Out of his view, Cole crawls along the edge of the water. Pain from his new gunshot wound digs through his abdomen like spikes. He pictures Lacey's face, and the image of his daughter's little face on the ultrasound, and battles through the agony.

He climbs the hill a few feet, the silhouette of the second terrorist coming into view. The man leans against a tree, aiming his light the opposite direction, as if still looking for Cole by the roll marks. His pistol arm seems ready to shoot at any trace of movement.

Cole feels around with the branch for indented snow, the guy's foot tracks. Once he finds them, he sneaks toward his opponent. Cole gets closer, about eight feet away. Then five. He reaches into his pocket and wraps his fingers around something.

Just before his next step lands, Gemento's slapping against the water stops, as if he's running out of energy. The woods go quiet. Cole's foot hits the snow with an audible crunch.

The second terrorist spins around. The flashlight brings out the stubble of his beard. His eyes widen. His gun arm straightens. Right before he lines up a shot, Cole jumps at him and stakes the pointy end of Diaz's metal surfboard into his jugular.

A gurgling sound sputters out of the guy's mouth. The phone falls, its light hitting him from the ground at a partial angle. Blood pours out of his neck. In the dimness, it looks black.

The guy remains on his feet, still trying to point the gun with a quaking hand. Cole rips it away and blasts a bullet through his temple. His wide body plops onto the phone, the light disappearing.

Cole kicks the heavy corpse to the side, picks up the phone, and shines it at the pond. All that's visible of Gemento is an arm, reaching up from the abyss onto a jagged sheet of ice at the pond's edge. In a couple seconds, his head appears, and both his arms slide about the icy block, as if trying to climb it. He fails, his head vanishing back into the water. He may soon lack the strength to even hang onto the block at all.

Cole tears off his sweatshirt, the cold biting harder at him in just a tee shirt. He tugs on the collar of the dead terrorist's tuxedo jacket, then maneuvers his thick arm out of the tight sleeve. The man's bloody head flops around. Cole yanks the jacket off the guy's other arm and ties the end of one sleeve onto the end of a sweatshirt sleeve.

He puts the pistol in his jeans' waist and, with the flashlight, negotiates the hill down to the pond, staying in already-made tracks in the snow. "William," he yells. "I'm coming."

Cole positions himself at the edge of the pond, just on the other side of the chunk of ice Gemento, AKA William, has been failing to climb. Cole wedges the lit-up phone in the snow and casts the tied-together jacket and sweatshirt out to William. It drapes the ice.

"You need to jump up just one more time," Cole shouts. "And grab the rope."

A few moments pass, no reaction. Cole debates venturing out onto the slab and grabbing him, but doesn't want his added weight to cave it in, trapping them underneath the heavy pieces. He watches William's still fingers.

An even larger slab creeps toward him. It would obliterate his arm. He'd go under and never get out. It's fewer than ten seconds away.

"Come on," Cole yells.

Five seconds left.

"You still have a son," Cole screams.

A loud gasp fills the woods.

William's head reappears. His healthy arm brushes over the ice. He gets hold of the sweatshirt. Planting his boots, Cole leans back and heaves William's torso up onto the slab. Though the bullet in Cole's side hit nothing vital, he's bleeding quite a lot and doesn't have much energy left himself. He pulls the rope again. William's hip lifts to the ice. His shivering legs meet the top just before the larger block demolishes them.

The rumble from the slab crash causes him to let go of the makeshift rope, causing Cole to stagger backward. William crawls toward him. He slips a bit, but reaches ground, and collapses in exhaustion near Cole's feet.

Cole pats him down. If he had a gun, he must've lost it on his way down the hill or in the water. Cole drops to the snow beside him. The forest is silent other than the sound of their heavy breath.

55

Cole sits up from the snowy ground, while soaked William still lies down, trembling and panting. Cole unties the two sleeves of the makeshift rope, wraps the tux jacket around his lower torso to control the gunshot bleeding, and slips his sweatshirt back on for heat.

"You saved my life," William says, his voice weak. His breaths are jerky, fast ones mixed with slow.

"Well, I had an ulterior motive. Lacey. My fiancee. You need to call it off."

William glances at the pistol at Cole's waist, then at his own bloody shoulder. "Is this bad?"

"You need to get to a doctor."

"I've never been shot before. It really hurts."

"I know. Your friend just shot me."

"Is Nate..."

"He's gone."

William wheezes, coughs, and wheezes again. Cole stands and extends his hand down. William gazes at it for a moment and grabs it. His hair is pressed flat from the water. The strands on his forehead look like tattoos.

"Are the cops still at the hotel?" William asks, a touch of sarcasm in his tone, like he already knows the answer.

"Yes."

William dips his head back, closes his eyes, and spreads his arms. He lets snowflakes collect on his face and open palms. He stays like this, without speaking.

"You're going to spend the rest of your life in prison," Cole says. "That new beginning you told me about over the phone, it isn't happening."

William's mouth forms a small smile. It's not a defiant one, as if to suggest he'll somehow beat a prison sentence. It has a sense of irony to it. The snow continues to build on his face and palms.

"From now until we get to the hotel will be the last of your life as a free man," Cole says. "What you make of that time is up to you. The way I see it, you have two choices. One, you can let your guy who kidnapped my fiancee hurt her. It won't get you the money. It'll just create more pain. Or, you can tell your guy to let her go. You may not have a new beginning, but you still have your reputation as a father. I imagine your son's opinion of you isn't very high after tonight. Killing an innocent pregnant woman will make it worse. Freeing her will make it better."

William's eyes remain closed for over half a minute. Then they open. "Okay."

A sense of relief runs through Cole's aching body. "Thank you, William."

"Will. My whole life, people called me Will."

"Thank you, Will."

When Cole patted him down, he didn't feel a phone, which must've fallen out of a pocket, so unlocks his own and hands it to him. Will logs into an encrypted file-storage platform and pulls up a list of numbers beside names. He scrolls to *Dale* and dials. Cole taps the speaker-mode button.

"Who is this?" a suspicious male voice asks on the other line.

"It's me," Will says. "Drop her off near her house, leave the truck, and call one of our guys to pick you up and get you out of Timber Ridge."

"He sent back the money?"

"No."

The phone is silent for a few seconds. "You're giving up?"

Will gazes at the dark, icy water. "I suppose I gave up a while ago."

He ends the call. A reflexive chuckle sneaks out of his mouth. He chuckles again, louder. Cole watches him laugh for a while. Then Cole points at the snowmobile on the hill. They climb toward it, Will leading the way along a bomb-free path, making noises that sometimes sound like laughing, sometimes crying.

When they reach the vehicle, Cole removes a zip-tie from the tux jacket and binds Will's hands behind his back, just to be sure he doesn't try anything. Cole sits on the front seat, Will the back, and drives toward the Alpine Grand.

The potent wind blows snowflakes on a diagonal and sends the ends of thinner tree branches into a quiver. The shadows of small animals dart into and out of the outer portions of the headlight beams. In the distance, to the left and right, the lightness of the snow and darkness of the night seem to merge into one color Cole couldn't quite name.

A couple minutes into the journey, Will says, "It's nice out here. The forest."

Cole, lightheaded from blood loss, isn't certain how to even respond to that comment in this moment.

"If you and I met in a different lifetime, like two hundred years ago, I think we may have ended up being good friends," Will says.

Cole thinks about this as the snowmobile engine buzzes. But again, he doesn't know how to reply.

Soon, the lights of the Alpine Grand shine on the other side of tall, snow-covered evergreens. Will directs Cole onto a no-bomb path to the front entrance. Holding Will's healthy arm, Cole leads him inside. The lobby's bright lights sting Cole's eyes. His cut one waters even more than it's been.

A SWAT cop near the Four Foxes Cafe turns around to the sound of their footsteps. His posture straightens with surprise at the sight of the bloody duo.

"He's Gemento," Cole says.

The cop rushes over and seizes Will. Cole, who realizes Will was helping hold him up, drops to a knee. He sways for a moment, then falls to the floor unconscious near the broken remains of the sculpture, *West Ward*.

56

Cole lies in a hospital bed in a shadowy room at Bozeman General, hooked up to an IV machine sending fluids and medicine into his body. A doctor cleaned, sealed, and bandaged both his gunshot wounds and gave him medicated drops for his right eye. He feels better than earlier, yet his body still hums with pain, and his sight still isn't all back. Different shapes of light shine on him and the walls as the national-news report jumps from shot to shot on the TV.

HOSTAGES EVACUATED stretches across the screen of a popular cable channel. The volume off, the newscaster speculates about what happened at the Alpine Grand tonight via closed caption. In a box beside him, aerial footage of the hotel rolls. It shows SWAT officers escorting a line of hostages out of the resort. The shot cuts to a hostage in the street being interviewed.

Will Laud, who's handcuffed to a bed somewhere in this hospital, gave police the location of the explosives. Cole recalls their time together in the forest. In particular, that thing Will said about them being good friends if they were around two hundred years ago. Though Cole gave the comment some thought then, he didn't form a full opinion. Now he does. Though the idea of being friends with a murderer who kidnapped his fiancee seems absurd, Cole can't rule out the possibility.

Will, of course, had the potential for destruction inside him. But, in a different time, if his land wasn't taken and his wife wasn't killed, that destructiveness could've stayed dormant. Will's friends, nor even Will himself, would've known it were there.

"The chief wants to give you a medal," a familiar voice says from the doorway.

Cole looks at the Black woman with the parka stuffed under her arm. Shauna. Though he's spoken to her a lot tonight, he hasn't seen her till now.

"They should give you the medal," he says.

She grins, then walks toward him. "I came to tell you the Gallatin County Sheriff's Office just got here with Lacey. She was a bit shook up, as you'd imagine, but health-wise, she's fine. She's on her way up."

Cole takes a deep breath.

"How you feeling?" Shauna asks.

"Physically, all right."

"Non-physically?"

He looks away, at the closed blinds over the window. "After getting back to the hotel, I passed out. Then woke up sometime later in an ambulance. In between, I had a dream."

"What kind of dream?"

"About my dad. My biological one, who died a while ago. In it, I was a boy. Maybe three or four. And we were in a room. It wasn't a room from the house I grew up in. It seemed older. But it somehow felt familiar, like him and I had both been there before. And my dad put a little white rabbit in my hands. Like the one on the jobsite, but it wasn't hurt. I liked it. It was mine. Then it jumped away. I tried to pick it up, but I couldn't get to it. It hopped out the door and didn't come back."

She stares at the TV, however, doesn't seem to be paying attention to the words on the screen. "What do you think it means?"

"I don't know."

"Just...get some rest."

"You think Lacey is going to forgive me?"

She adjusts the parka under her arm. "That's between you and her."

The room is quiet for a while, until a knock on the open door. Lacey stands in the doorway. She wears snow boots, leggings, a puffy winter coat, and a beanie with a pom over her uncombed hair. She doesn't smile.

"I'll give you two some privacy," Shauna says. She seems to sense Lacey's anger at Cole. Shauna leans over the bed and hugs him, careful to not interfere with his bandages or IV. "Keep in touch."

"I will."

On her way out the door, she nods at Lacey, then disappears down the hallway. Lacey stares at Cole with her arms folded, as if waiting for him to say something. Behind her, a nurse pushes by a woman in a wheelchair.

"I'm so sorry," Cole says.

Lacey remains in the doorway, the heavy shadow on the floor separating them. "The cops told me about the terrorists at the hotel. I've accepted that you...involve yourself in things like that. Though I resisted it at first, I'd be lying if I said it didn't appeal to me on some level. I know you mean well. When the retaliation comes my direction, I don't like it, of course, but I can handle it. I'm an adult." Lacey pats her stomach. "She isn't."

He closes his eyes, nods, and rubs his temples.

"Our child winding up at the center of some deadly threat, is this something I'm going to have to worry about for the rest of my life?" she asks.

He considers his response for a while. "That picture of you was the worst thing I ever saw. If I'm ever in a situation again that could even possibly put our baby in danger, I'll be reminded of what I felt tonight when I looked at that picture. And I'll listen to that instinct. I can't predict the future. But I can promise you I'll try my best to never let anything like this happen again."

Though her expression is still serious, a subtle smile breaks onto it. She points at the TV. Another freed hostage is giving an interview. His closed-caption response mentions *some man who came out of nowhere and looked out for all of us.*

"When you try your best at things, like this at the hotel, usually you get them done," Lacey says. "No matter how stressful the circumstances. I would have to believe that's going to stay the same for your daughter. As mad as I was tonight, I think you're going to be a good dad."

"Yeah?"

"Yeah."

The tension in his shoulders eases. He grins. She jogs toward his bed, the pom on her hat flopping around, and they kiss.

"I love you," he says.

"I love you too."

57

Governor Hampton, in a black suit with a red pocket square, taps his fingers on the leather mat of the desk in his office. The calamity at the hotel ended three days ago. He still has a couple bruises from the stampede out of the ballroom, but the damage could've been much harsher. The nationwide revolution the Children of the Sun called for never happened. Social-media users praised Hampton's resilience for surviving. The incident was shaping up to be a boon for his image. Until this morning.

His TV is tuned into a business-news cable channel. A table of four commentators have been discussing an upcoming announcement, set for 11:00 AM, from the CEO of Stallos Energy, Rose Stallos. Rumors are that the announcement will be big, with major implications on the stock. Hampton tried contacting her multiple times this morning, via email, text, and call, to figure out what the hell she was about to say, but she hasn't responded.

His assistant appears in the doorway. On a nearby shelf is a statue shaped like fire, which helps Hampton think positive thoughts, so he can manifest positive outcomes.

"Hi, sir," she says. "On the line I have Martin O'Brien, from the Parkinson's awareness—"

"Tell him to fuck off. I'm busy."

She nods and disappears.

The time changes to 11:00 AM and the news channel cuts to a live feed of a podium outside the Stallos Energy headquarters. The unpictured commentators keep speaking, speculating. In a couple minutes, Rose walks into the frame and the commentators hush. The TV is silent besides the click of cameras from photographers in front of the podium.

Rose lowers the microphone a couple inches. "It's been both a pleasure and honor to be the CEO of Stallos Energy. I've had the privilege of working alongside some of the brightest, most dedicated people on earth. However, at this juncture, I feel the company would be better served under the leadership of a new chief executive officer. Which is why I'm resigning from my position, effective immediately."

Within seconds, the text at the bottom of the screen changes from *ROSE STALLOS ANNOUNCEMENT* to *ROSE STALLOS RESIGNATION*.

"Stallos Energy has always been an exemplar of corporate ethics," she says. "Honesty, forthrightness, and accountability are just some of the company's many values. I have not been honest and forthright. However, with my resignation, I am hoping to at least be considered accountable. At the advice of my attorneys, I cannot go into detail, however, I will say that I engaged in unethical practices on a recent project. This decision was not made by the Stallos staff. It was made by me. To them, and anyone else affected, I apologize."

She walks away from the podium. Reporters shout questions at her, which she does not answer. The screen cuts back to the commentators around the table. They don't speak for a moment, all with surprised expressions.

"A bombshell of an announcement from Stallos Energy

CEO...former CEO...Rose Stallos," an Asian man with a shiny tie says on TV.

"You can't help but make a connection to the hostage ordeal last Friday," a black-haired woman with gold earrings says. "On livestream, the terrorists asked her, and Montana governor Grant Hampton, to make a confession about a pipeline. Did we just get that confession?"

"A version of it, it seems. With that bit about her lawyers, she didn't say enough to incriminate herself, but certainly enough to tarnish her reputation."

"If she made an admission like this the other night, a part of you would have to consider that it were made because she was under duress. That it might not be true, that she was just trying to appease her captors. But for her to come out and say something like this today, with the terrorists all dead or in prison, makes you believe it."

As the commentators hypothesize about what Rose meant by "unethical practices," Hampton springs off his tufted leather chair and closes his door. He doesn't want his assistant, or any other staff, to hear this call.

He dials the number of the private-wealth investment banker in Manhattan who manages his family's timber fortune. Though the shrewd banker is fantastic with money, his Machiavellian worldview is handy for political advice, too.

"I just watched it," the banker says.

"I was standing next to that bitch on video at the hotel. We were a...you know, a package. Her admitting guilt is going to—"

"You look guilty, too."

"Even if I deny it. This can wreck my run at the White House." With a shaky hand, Hampton reaches for a glass of water and knocks it over, wetting his hardwood floor.

"You need more than your word to beat this."

The banker outlines a solution to the problem. Hampton likes it. When the call ends, he tells his assistant to come in with paper towels. He listens to music through headphones as she dries up the mess on her knees.

Late that night, he drives out to an empty field in Helena, no buildings in sight. Soon, the headlights of a second car appear on the horizon. The Ford Focus turns off the asphalt onto the field. Though the blizzard stopped Saturday morning, the ground is still snowy, the car leaving tracks as it approaches Hampton's black Mercedes.

Vern Sanders, the droopy-faced, sixty-one-year-old head of Montana's Department of Environmental Quality, steps out of the Ford in a bland jacket and walks to Hampton's driver's door as the window rolls down.

After Ollie poisoned the water of Laud Farm, Vern and his team were tasked with investigating the infraction and issuing fines. They were not informed that the water was contaminated by an outside source, as part of a ploy to boot William Laud off his land. They were just doing their jobs.

Hands buried in his pockets, Vern looks around at the barren location. He seems anxious. "What is this about?"

"Chill out, Vern. Something good is about to happen to you." Hampton holds up a thumb drive. "There's five million dollars of Bitcoin on here. It's yours, if you do everything I'm about to tell you."

58

The live band plays a cover of The Rolling Stones' "Tumbling Dice" at Rodney's Rock House, a new bar in Timber Ridge. Cole sits at a table near the stage. His body is still sore in places, and his eyesight still a touch blurry, but he's healing well two weeks after the Alpine Grand crisis. His doctor tells him he'll have a full recovery soon.

He turned the $2.725 million of Bitcoin over to police, who distributed it back to the robbed Stallos Energy employees. Eagle, a recipient, wanted to thank Cole for all he did at the hotel by treating him to a fancy dinner with as many guests as he'd like. Instead, Cole opted for this place, known for its burgers and wings.

At Cole's table is Lacey, who'll just drink club soda, his brother Jay, Jay's wife, Shauna, and Diaz, who was given back his little surfboard. Diaz seems to be healing well, too. He decided to take online classes and get his real-estate license. He's been chatting with Lacey, about her online classes for psychology.

Eagle walks into Rodney's Rock House with a grin. Next week, he has a lunch date with his coworker Breann. He waves and approaches the table. Weaving through the crowd, he passes neon beer-logo displays on the wall and a pair of large antlers with hats hanging from them, a Santa one, a Viking one, and a chef one, among others. People shoot Eagle funny glances. Not just because of the large splint on his nose, but because of his designer loafers, which he wears without socks in ten-degree weather. He doesn't seem bothered by the looks.

Cole greets him with a hand slap and introduces him to everyone at the table he hasn't yet met. Eagle studies Jay's face for a moment and says, "Holy shit. Are you What Do You Say Jay?"

Jay glimpses Cole and says, "You screwing with me? You tell him to say that?"

"No." He's telling the truth.

"Those videos have reached a good amount of people, babe," Jay's wife says. "For better or worse." She chuckles. So does Lacey.

"I caught the new one this morning," Eagle says, "about added fees during online purchases. It was funny, man."

Jay's chest puffs with pride. "It's been a journey. But I think I've really come into my own as an internet icon."

His wife rolls her eyes.

The group orders food. After everyone eats, Lacey saunters to the dance floor and waves over the others. Diaz remains seated, understandable with the leg injury, but everyone else joins her and starts dancing. Eagle brings a lot of energy, getting up on his toes in the loafers while spinning his fists around each other.

After a couple songs, Shauna leans to Cole and says above the music, "Another cop just sent me this." She hands him her phone, an article on the screen from a state-news site. The headline, *Vern Sanders, Head of DEQ, Steps Down.*

Cole focuses on a quote from Vern Sanders, *"Rose Stallos's statement urged me to admit the state government's participation in the 'unethical practices' she referenced. Out of respect for her,*

I will not go into any detail. However, I will admit that I behaved in a shameful way, too. This decision on behalf of the DEQ was only mine. My staff was not involved, nor was the leadership of the state government. I especially apologize to Governor Hampton, whom the Children of the Sun falsely targeted for unethical behavior that was not his, but mine."

One eyebrow raised, Shauna appears skeptical about the article. Cole shakes his head while passing her back the phone. Something about the story feels a bit too convenient for Hampton.

Cole tries to not let this bother him. He played his part in the Alpine Grand incident by saving as many hostages as he could. If Hampton did something unscrupulous to have that article published, Cole isn't responsible for exposing it. As long as humans are on this planet, it will have corruption. Cole can't try to fix every problem out there.

In a few minutes, Eagle leans to him and says, "Yo, wanted to give you a heads-up. I spoke to my dad. He can get your daughter a spot in that preschool. If you want it, you got to let me know ASAP, though. With the big waitlist, they can't hold it for long."

To afford top-tier private schools from preschool on, Cole would have to get a second job. Though he can't fix every problem in the world, he does need to be around to fix his daughter's, in particular, those unexpected dilemmas Shauna warned him about. If he's out of the house working most days and nights of her childhood, she'd be missing out on all he could offer as a dad.

Last week, he and Lacey discussed their daughter's education. He'll contribute to a college fund from the moment she's born. Over the next eighteen years, he'll put aside enough from Maddox Construction to afford her full tuition at any university she may wish to attend, public or private, regardless of how expensive. Until then, Timber Ridge's public school system should be just fine.

"I appreciate it, Eagle," Cole says. "But we're going to send her somewhere local."

"No worries." Eagle shimmies away.

Cole's eyes meet Lacey's. He twirls her. While they dance, he places his hand over her stomach, and she smiles. Tonight, he thinks he'll have a good dream.

THANK YOU FOR READING FROZEN DREAM!

We hope you enjoyed it as much as we enjoyed bringing it to you. We just wanted to take a moment to encourage you to review the book. Follow this link: **Frozen Dream** to be directed to the book's Amazon product page to leave your review.

Every review helps further the author's reach and, ultimately, helps them continue writing fantastic books for us all to enjoy.

You can also join our non-spam mailing list by visiting www.subscribepage.com/AethonReadersGroup and never miss out on future releases. You'll also receive three full books completely Free as our thanks to you.

Facebook | Instagram | Twitter | Website

Looking for more great Thrillers?

T.J. BREARTON

THE DARK IS ALWAYS WAITING

A MIND-BENDING CRIME THRILLER

SMART AND SURPRISING AND FAST-PACED...
—LISA REGAN, AUTHOR OF VANISHING GIRLS

Stopping a tragedy makes him a hero... ...But was any of it real? After surviving a public shooting and saving someone in the process, Alex Baines's life is forever altered... Video of the tragic event spills across social media. Major newspapers are interested. Even movie deals are being offered. This could be a career boost for the neuroscientist and meditation guru. But Alex's marriage hangs on by a thread. His leg is shattered from a bullet wound. Evidence is piling up that the attack was not random. And while police hunt down the gunman, Alex's wife Corrine begins to worry someone is after her and her two children, too. All the while, state Investigator Raquel Roth has never seen a case like this. A criminal who makes major mistakes, yet seems to have a master plan. And is someone pulling his strings? As Roth and her partner race to figure out the madman's motive, signs point to an even more sinister plan in the works. If only they can untangle the mystery and stop the disaster in time...
"Smart and surprising and fast-paced...an excellent book. There were so many small moments in there that I really related to and were just brilliant. (Brearton is) a master at capturing the minutiae of a marriage."—Lisa Regan, author of Vanishing Girls *This book was previously published as Breathing Fire, but has been completely revised into this definitive version.

TED GALDI

Get The Dark is Always Waiting Now!

Sentenced to life in prison for a crime he didn't commit... Can he be exonerated? After ten years inside a jail cell, Andy Gibbons has abandoned all hope. Resigned himself to the fact that he will spend the rest of his life behind bars. But while Andy may have thrown in the towel, that doesn't mean his wife, Jamie, did. Disillusioned and worn out by the justice system, the Honorable Judge Regan St. Clair is just about to pack in too when a letter from Jamie Gibbons arrives on her desk. A letter that changes everything... Digging deeper, she and a former Special Forces operator named Jake Westley stumble into a frightening underworld of deceit and menace. A world where nothing is as it seems, and no one can be trusted. All the answer these simple question: *Is Andy Gibbons really innocent? Is the price of his freedom worth paying?* **Don't miss this** crime suspense-thriller about a corrupt organization with a sinister agenda that exploits every weakness and every dark corner of the fallible justice system.

Get Unguilty Now!

A deadly explosion rocks the nation's capital...
Three seemingly unconnected people – a British ex-Special Forces operative, an ex-Navy Seal, and a teenage girl – find themselves under suspicion for the attack. Soon, they're in the middle of a conspiracy that threatens to unsettle the entire United States. If they have any hope to survive the dangerous situation they've found themselves in, these strangers must learn to rely on each other, all while the question remains: Did one of *them* cause the explosion?
Nefarious organizations arrange themselves behind the political scenes. The players prepare their moves. An entire Country hangs in the balance. Can anyone stop them? Find out in this adrenaline-pumping action-thriller from bestseller Paul Heatley.

Get Sleeper Cell Now!

For all our Thrillers, visit our website.

Printed in Dunstable, United Kingdom